Written by Paul Wilson

Photography and Design by Chris Keys

Illustrations by Laura Tinald

Additional illustrations by Robert Herzig

ETHIOPI AID

Thank you. By enjoying this graphic novel, you have helped more children like Haikim win the race against a life of poverty.

For over 20 years, Ethiopiaid have been supporting the poorest people in Ethiopia. Your purchase will help our local partners in carrying out their life-saving work. Every day they put children into the classroom, protect women through childbirth and give men the skills they need to support their families.

We are supporting this creative project by ensuring that 25% of all profits are transferred directly to the people who need it most.

Find our more about our work and read about the difference you've made by visiting www.ethiopiaid.org.uk

Available on the App Store

www.e-motionpublishing.net/TheFlame
Also available as an animated graphic novel for ipad.

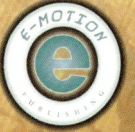

This is a work of fiction. Names, characters, businesses, places, events and incidents are either the products of the author's imagination or used in a fictitious manner. Any resemblance to actual persons, living or dead, or actual events is purely co-incidental.

Copyright 2012 e-motion publishing / Make Believe uk LTD.

Mostly, I can tell by the colours whether they believe or not. Believers have rich, vibrant colours burning inside. They carry a flame in the heart that sets them apart. Bekele, Gebrselassie and Dibaba burn crimson red, on fire, oh they really have it. But you already knew that.

I first spot them in their teens, that's when the fire rages and I can see them through space and time. Some burn brightly then fade, but believers are so bright it can blind me. They are funny at that age, crazy eyes some of them. Staring down competitors, blanking the crowd, sinking into the ground. So serious. I digress.

Haikim was different. I saw him before he was even born, burning up inside his mothers womb, pushing and kicking to get out. I've never seen colours like it, before or after. As a young child a ring of fire encircled him and most could see his gift. Of course, such things are passed down in search of one who believes. Like others, Haikim's flame remained close to home for a while, but unlike most, he was born in a storm and tested in greater ways.

I'm not one for science, religion or philosophy, I've seen far too much for that. But when I felt him running for the first time I cried. It was exhilarating. Over the years I have encountered your champions and what many call heroes. But it is much simpler and purer than that in my experience.
One thing sets believers apart.

The flame.

2 Days to race

Looking at him now, surrounded by all this pomp and ceremony makes this a rare story indeed.

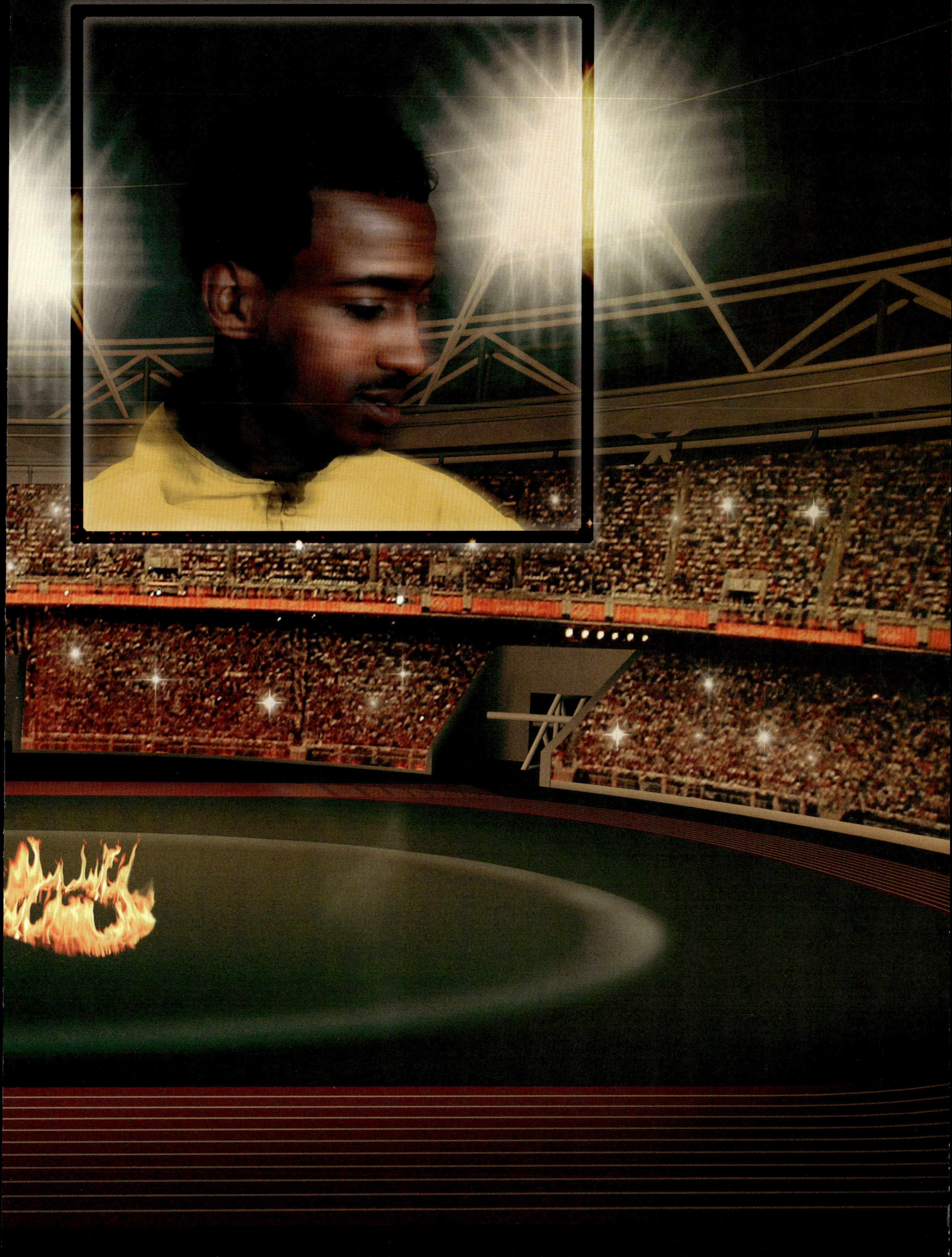

Same charms...

Same loyalties...

Same bare feet.

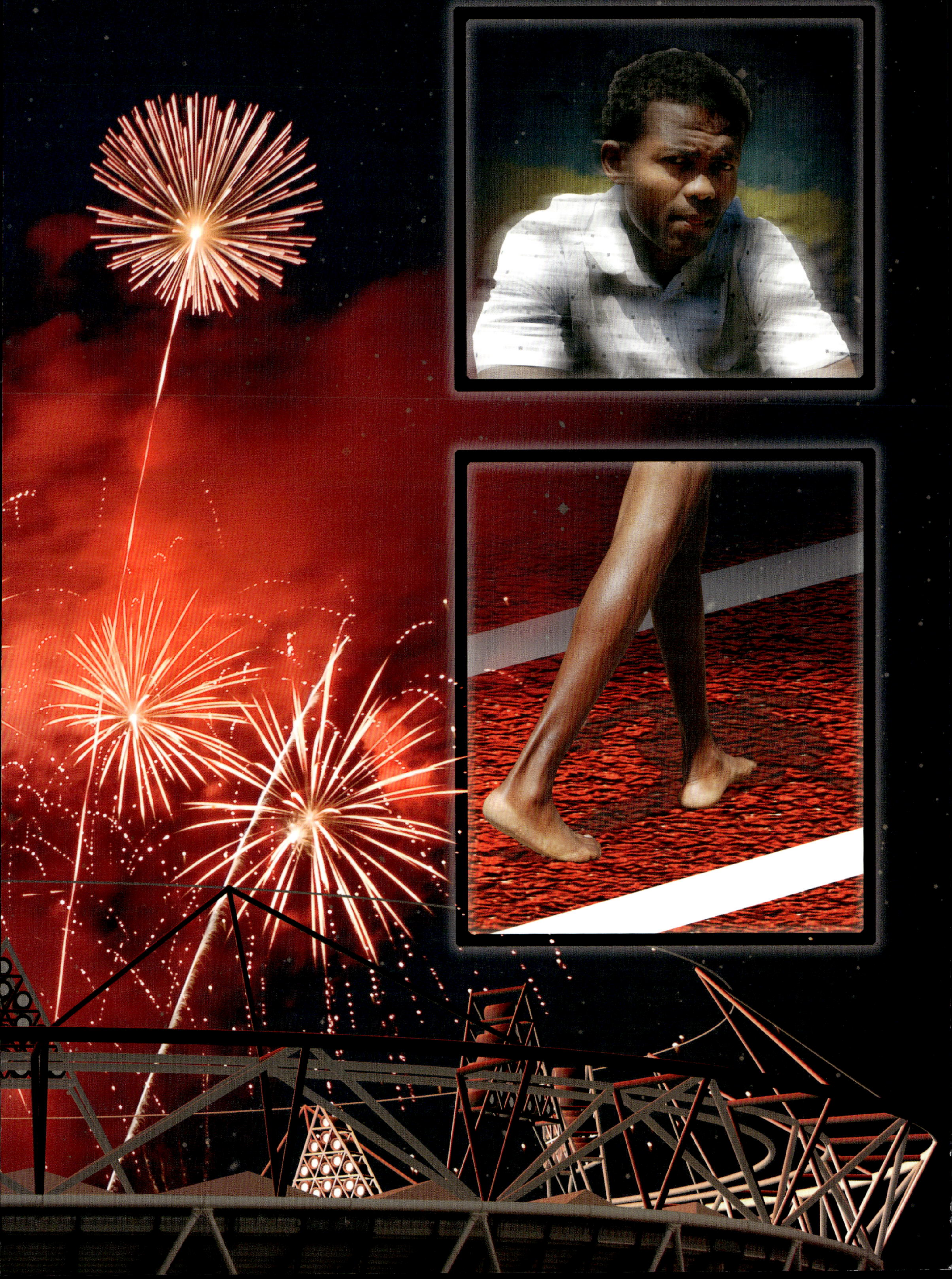

Great change occurs when the living overcome their fears. A flame born of belief burns brightest of all. When one believes in something so much that they can see, feel or hear it then possibility is alive. Fanning the flames is my role.

It is a blessing mortals do not share such perspective as most endeavours would surely never begin. What a crime that would be as most only experience eternity once or twice in a lifetime.

I however am condemned. I have already seen how this ends.

> **Wallo, Ethiopia**

Against such barren wastelands the flame is more easily extinguished than ignited. Yet down through aeons one truth has revealed itself to me more than once. All men have within them the seed of greatness inherited from the tree of life and forged over time.

This is life's gift to man. The gift is the flame.

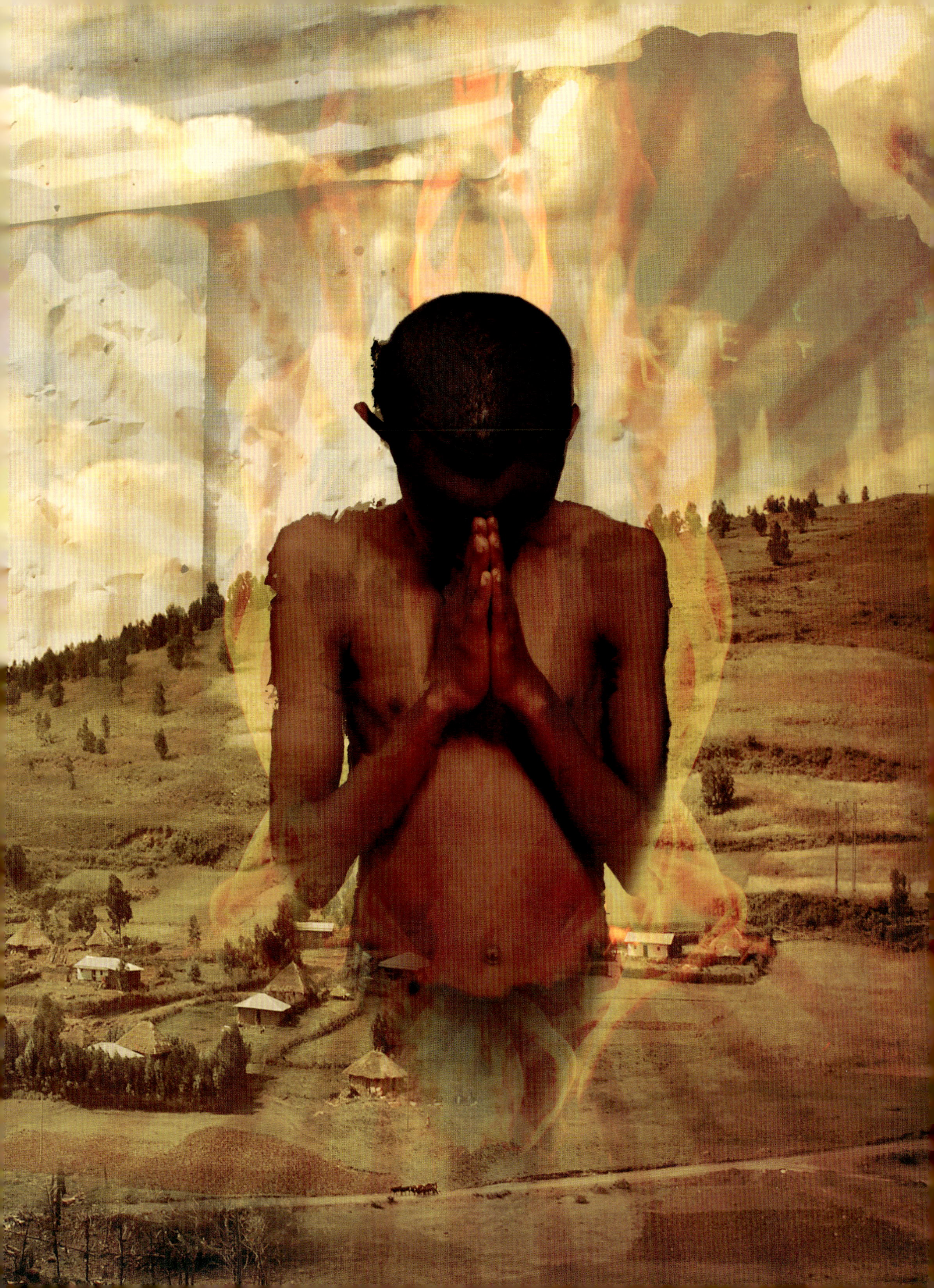

The arrival of buds was replaced at this time with the arrival of disaster and farmers to the camps. The rains had failed again and large parts of the land that men call Ethiopia was in drought.

Your wars raged on around the famine, crippling any help from the outside world.

Another year, another drought as the land split and cracked with the heat. The Southern Highlands had more than five million souls living on relief food. Emergency camps were overwhelmed and man's dark shadows emerged.

Before it ended over eight million people were famine victims and one million were lost.

The rest of the world watched in horror.

"Hell on Earth" their words not mine.

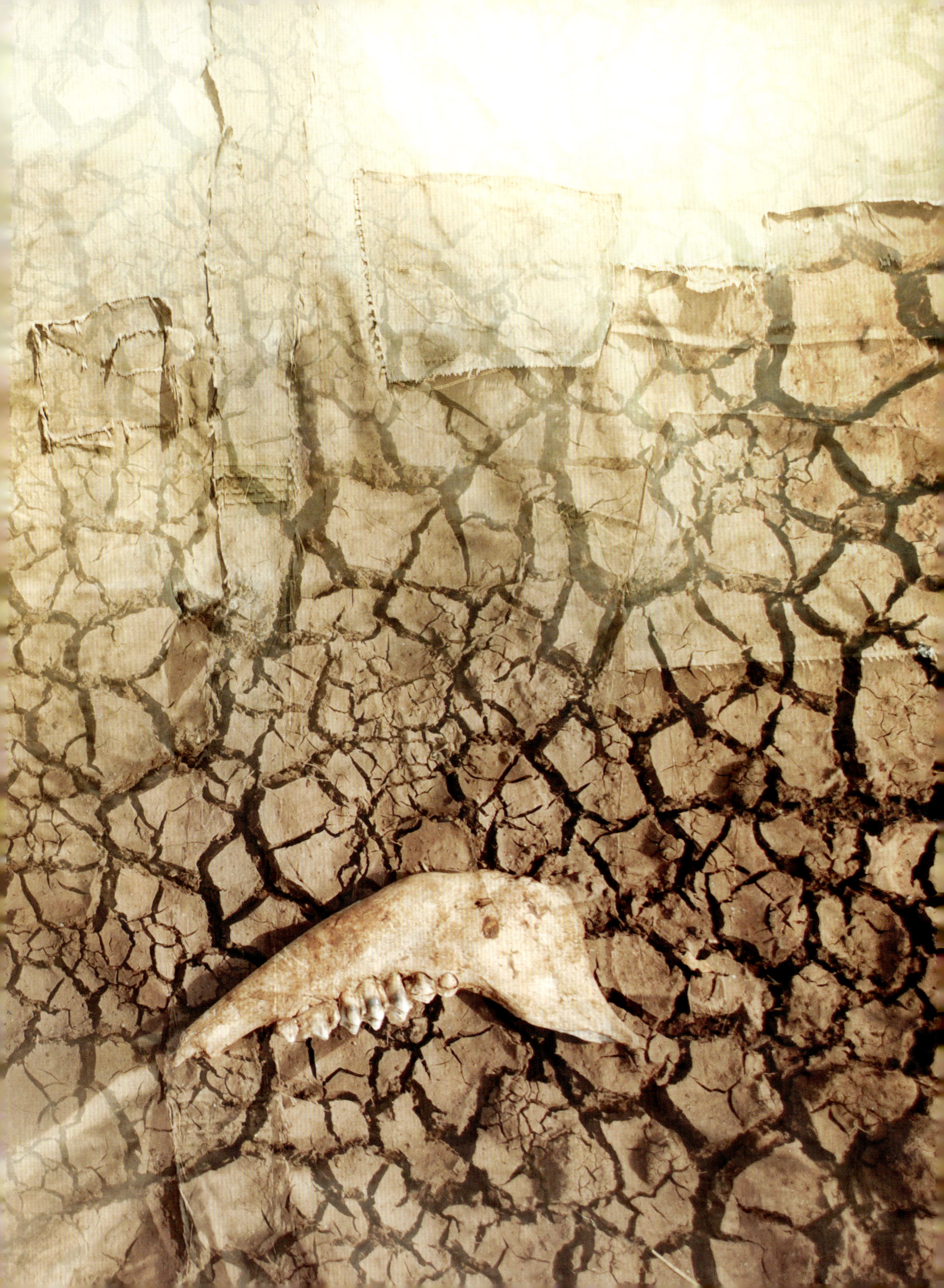

Like millions of others Haikim was born into poverty. Time is less a healer and more an anaesthetic that numbs your response to such things. The way of man, so full of inequality and deprivation will always remain a mystery to me. As will his spirit of survival.

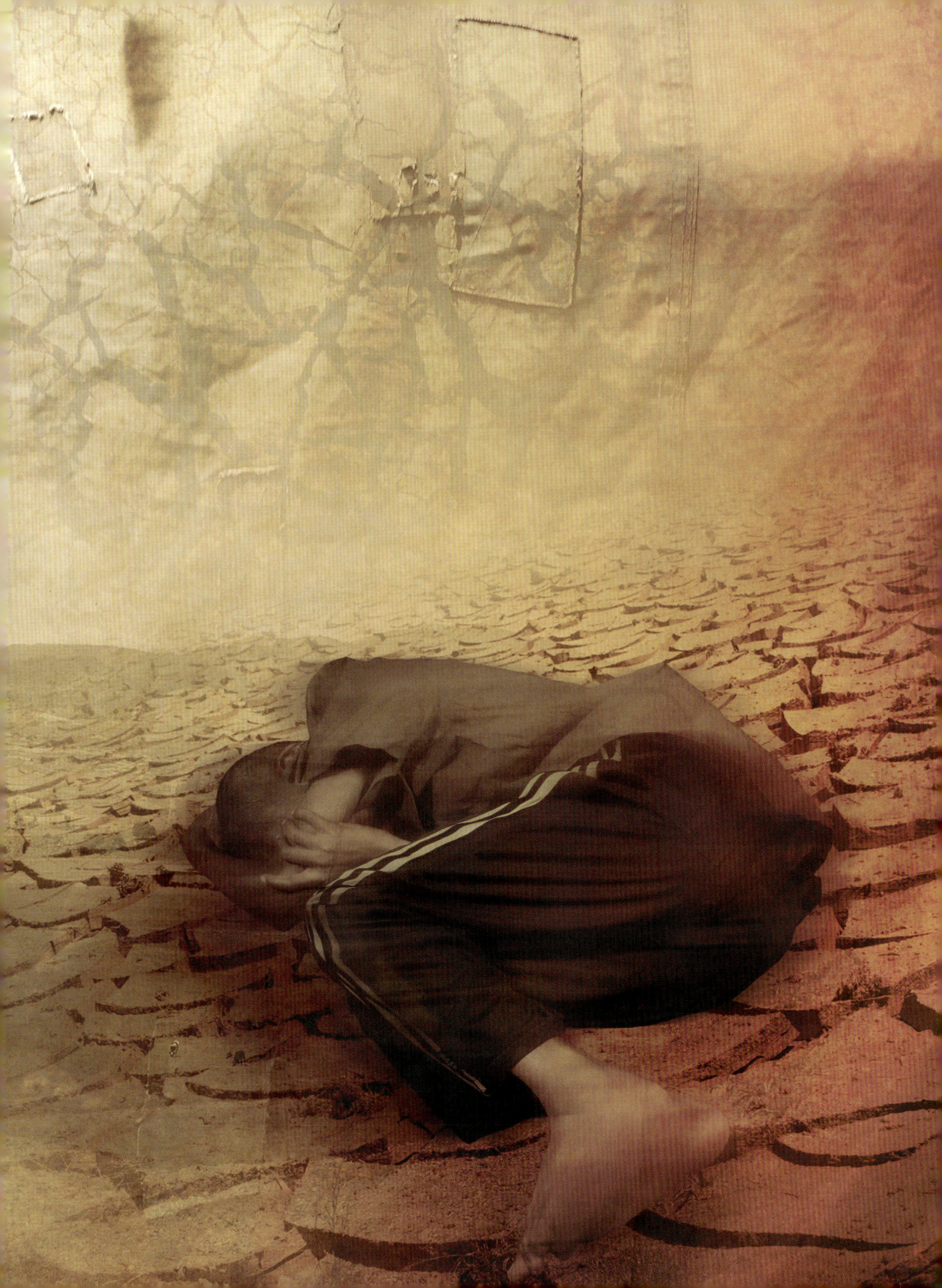

Stories can nourish the stomachs of the starving...

"HAIKIM, DO YOU BELIEVE IN DEMONS?"

ONCE THERE WAS A FATHER WITH SEVEN SPOILT CHILDREN.

HE WAS WORRIED THAT THEY WOULD GROW UP LAZY AND POOR AND WHEN THE ELDERS SPOKE OF A TERRIBLE DROUGHT TO THE NORTH HE DECIDED TO TEACH THEM A LESSON.

HE TOLD EACH CHILD IN SECRET THAT HE HAD BURIED ALL HIS TREASURE IN THE LAND AROUND THEIR HOME. THE RICHES IN THIS EARTH ARE GREATER THAN DIAMONDS, RUBIES OR GOLD HE TOLD THEM ONE BY ONE.

BEING GREEDY ALL THE CHILDREN DECIDED TO DIG UP THE LAND TO FIND THE TREASURE HE SPOKE OF. FOR MANY DAYS THEY DUG IN SECRET WITH STICKS, TOOLS AND EVEN THEIR BARE HANDS. THEY DUG HUNDREDS OF SMALL HOLES LOOKING, BUT COULD NOT FIND ANYTHING.

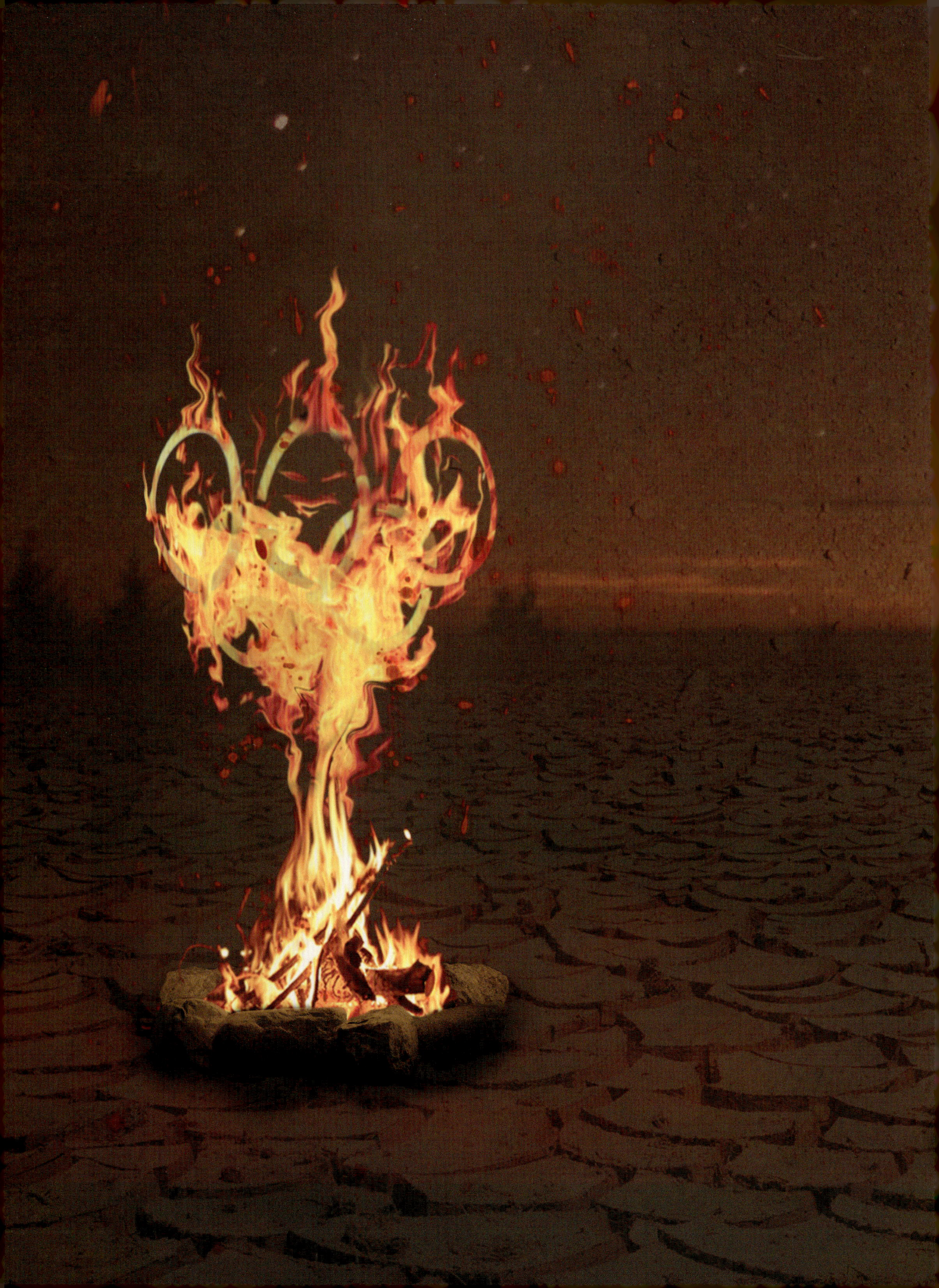

I'D RATHER HAVE DIAMONDS THAN SEEDS!
BE QUIET I'M TRYING TO LISTEN

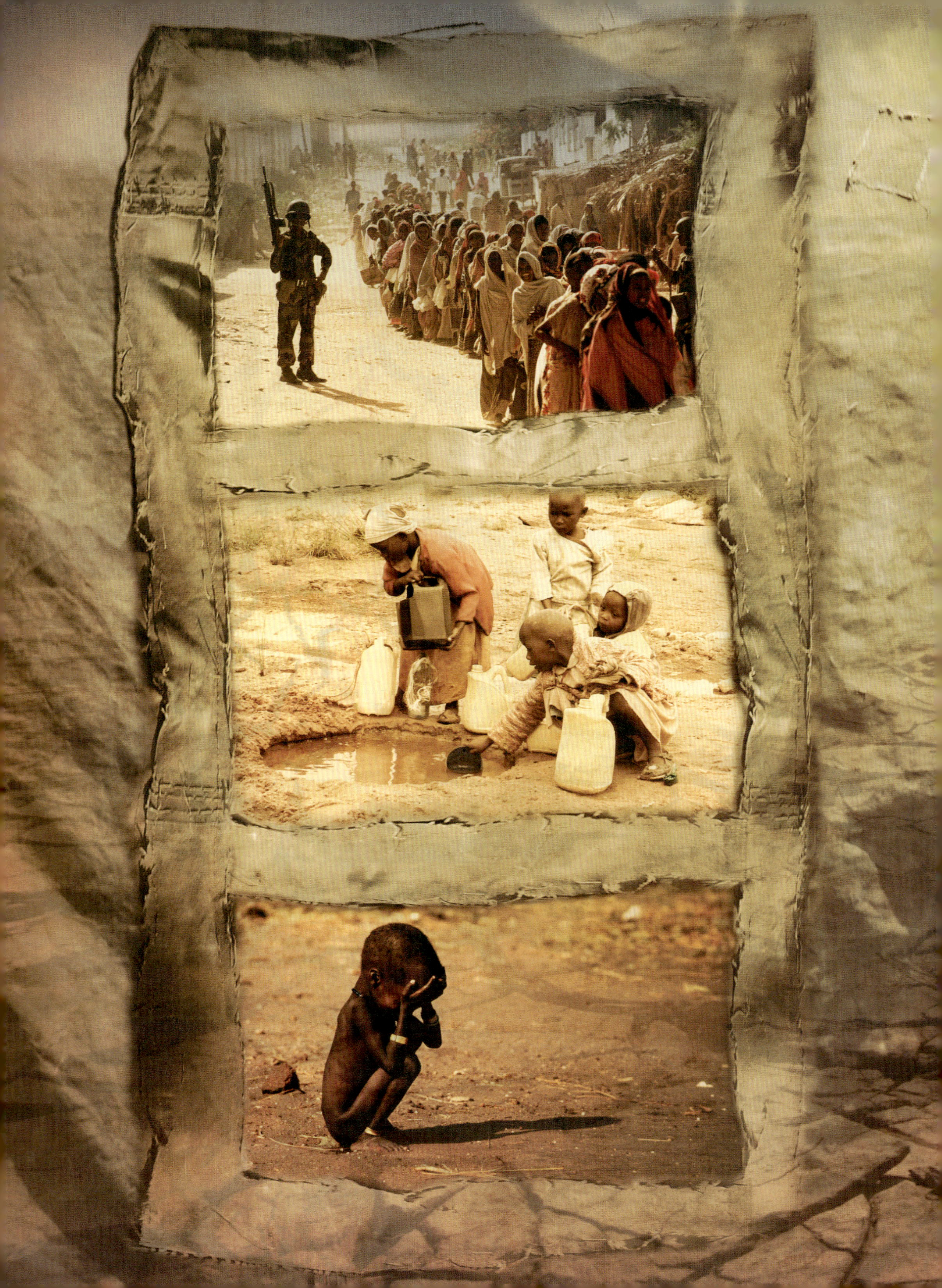

WHY MUST WE QUEUE ALL DAY?
STOP YOUR WHINING. WE ARE LUCKY TO HAVE FOOD.
THIS IS NOT FOOD, IT'S... WAIT WHAT IS THAT...?
IT'S A ROACH! LUCKY YOU!

ALL WE DO IS QUEUE AND WAIT...
QUEUE AND WAIT AND SIT...
...AND LISTEN TO STUPID STORIES.

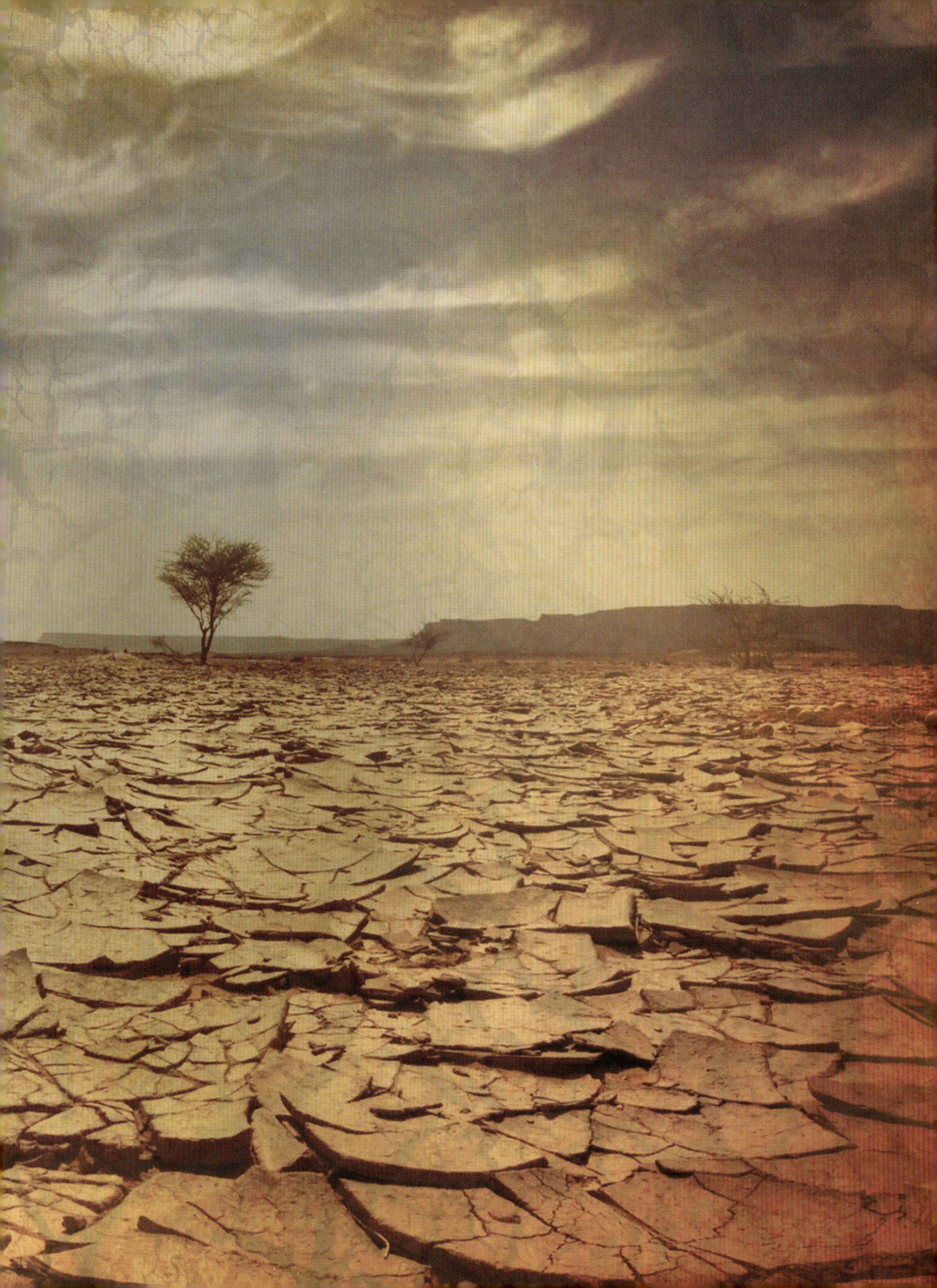

WHAT DID HE SAY?
HE SAID GOD LOVES US AND THAT WE SHOULDN'T LOSE FAITH
HMM, DID HE BRING BREAD TODAY?

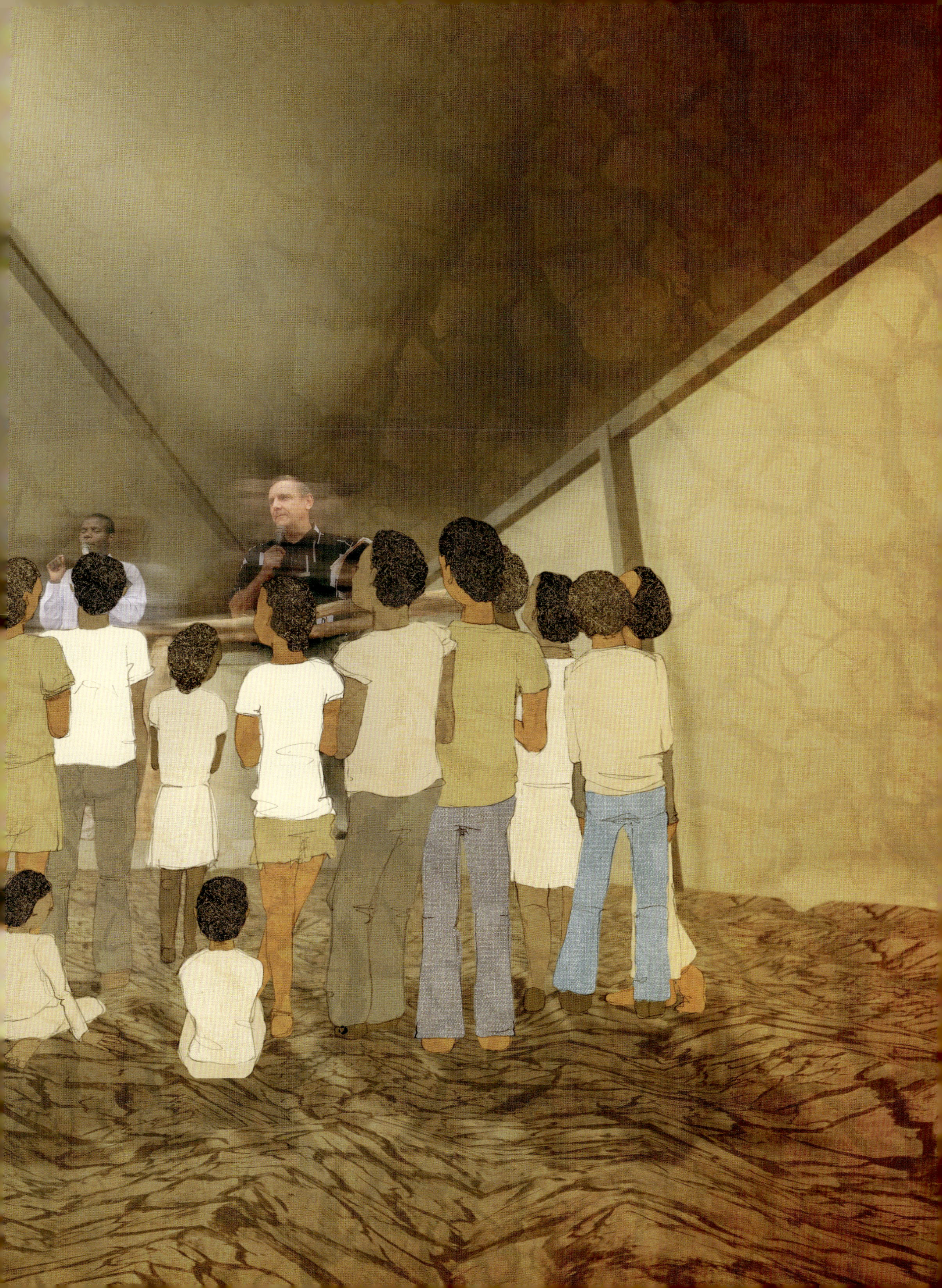

Only when everything is gone, do people discover spirit.
Sometimes rock bottom provides solid foundations.

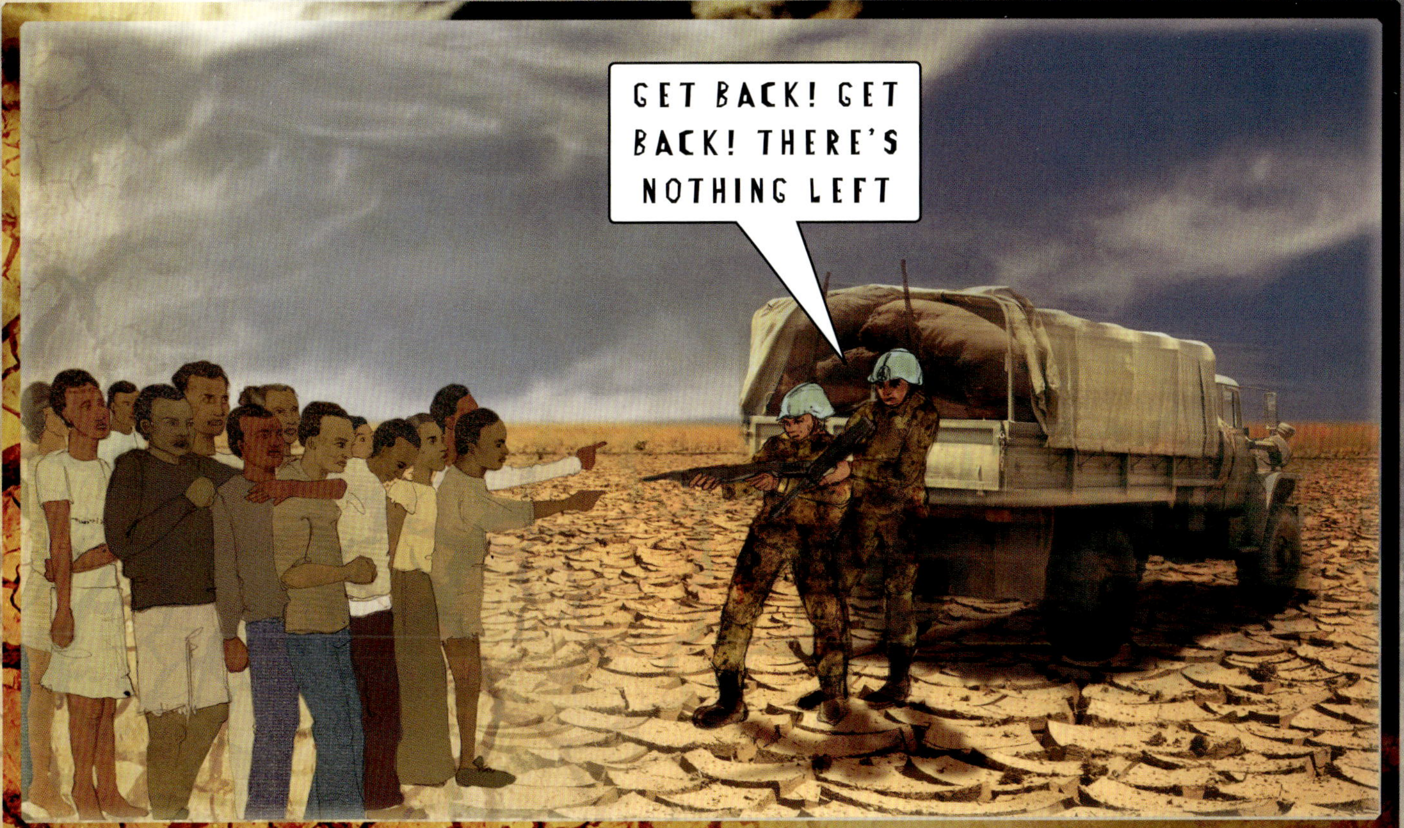
GET BACK! GET BACK! THERE'S NOTHING LEFT

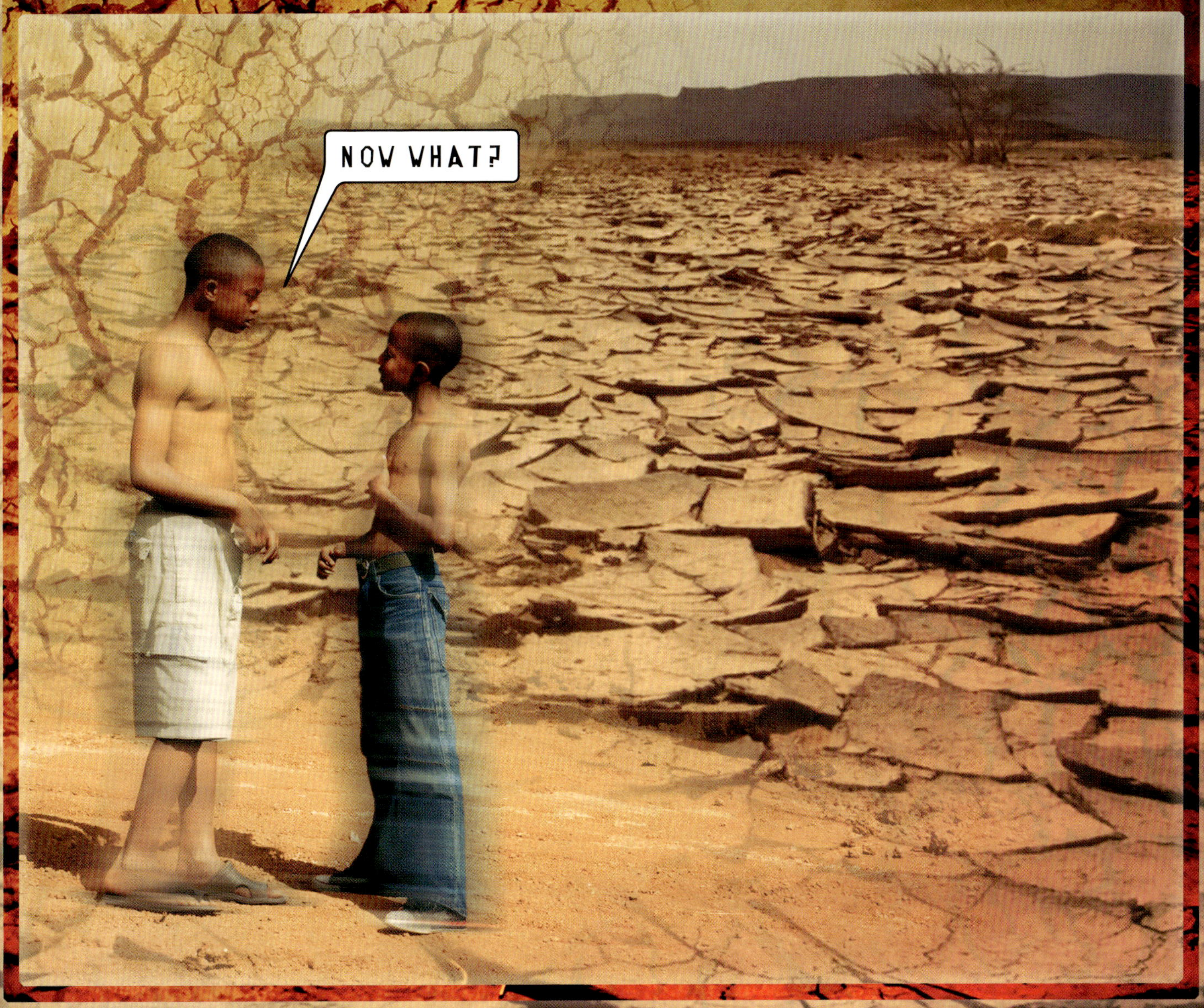
NOW WHAT?

2 Hours to 10km race

Giorgis
33
NO, IT'S NOT ON RIGHT
I WANT IT TIGHTER
IT'S AS TIGHT AS IT CAN BE

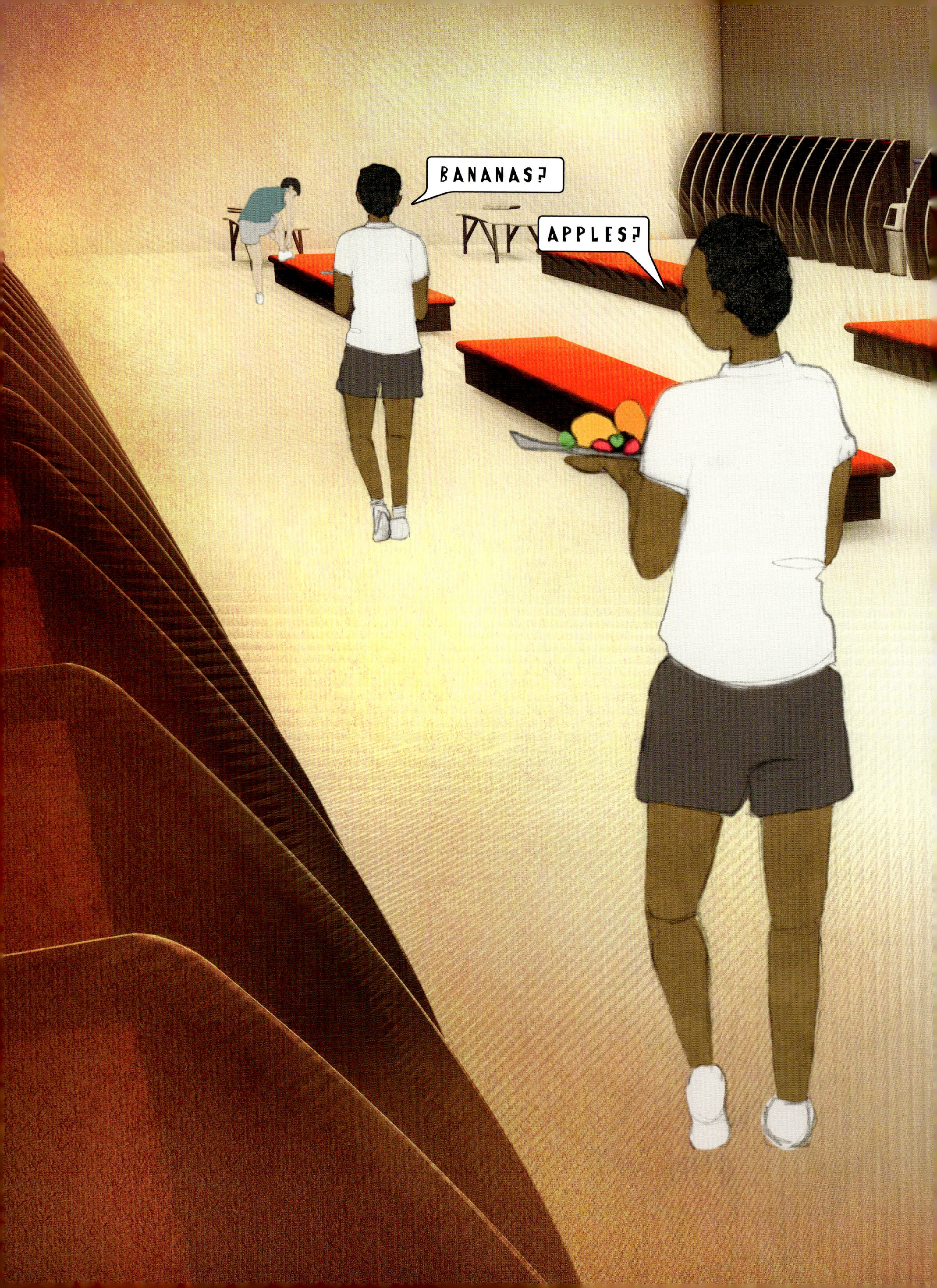
BANANAS?
APPLES?

MANGO? PAPAYA? LOOKIE?

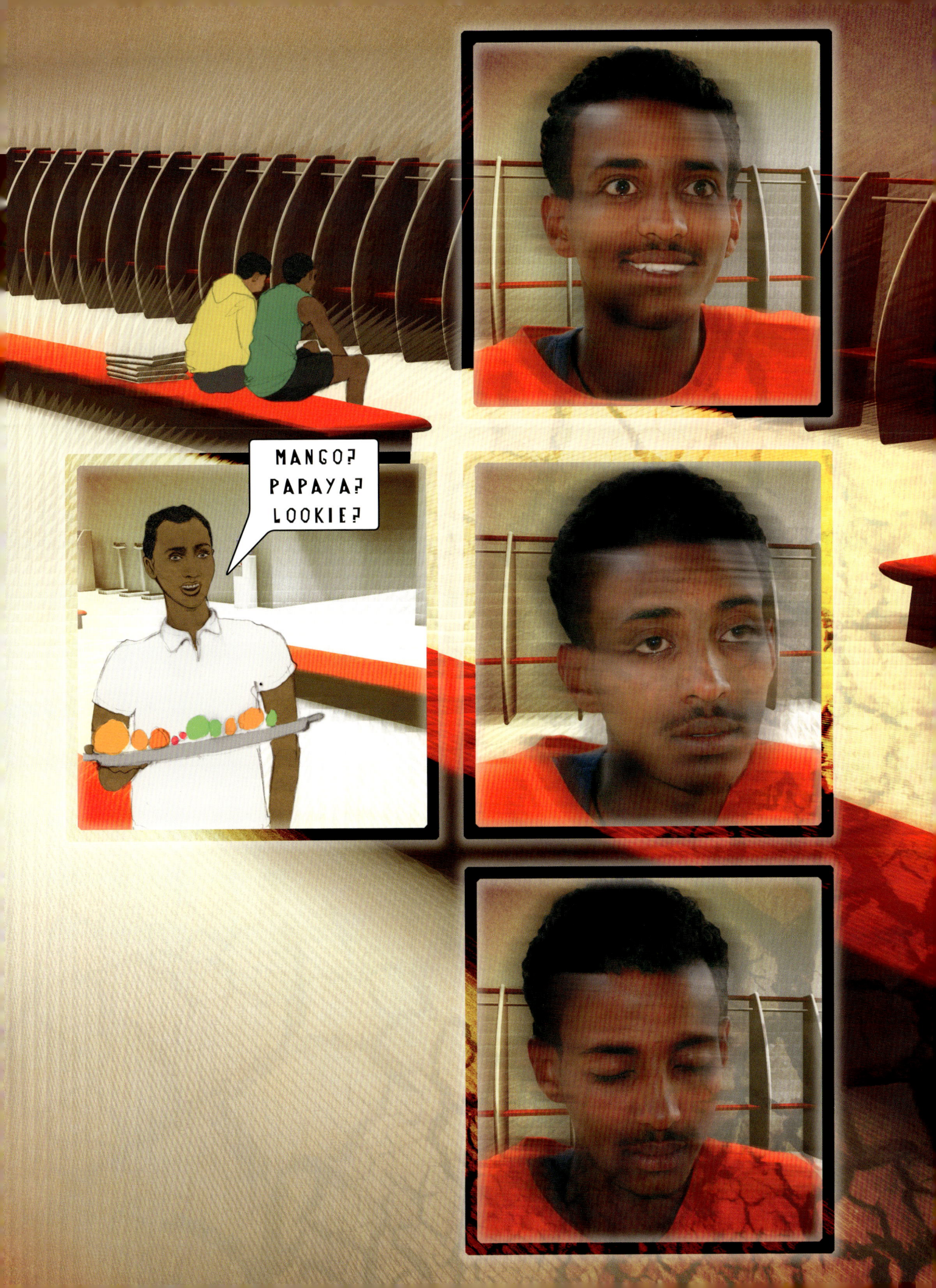

Ethiopia

YOU LOOK HUNGRY LITTLE ONES... HOW OLD ARE YOU? BROTHERS?
I'M HUNGRY! I AM KILLI AND I AM TEN. THIS IS HAIKIM HE'S SIX
WE'RE NOT HUNGRY THANK YOU

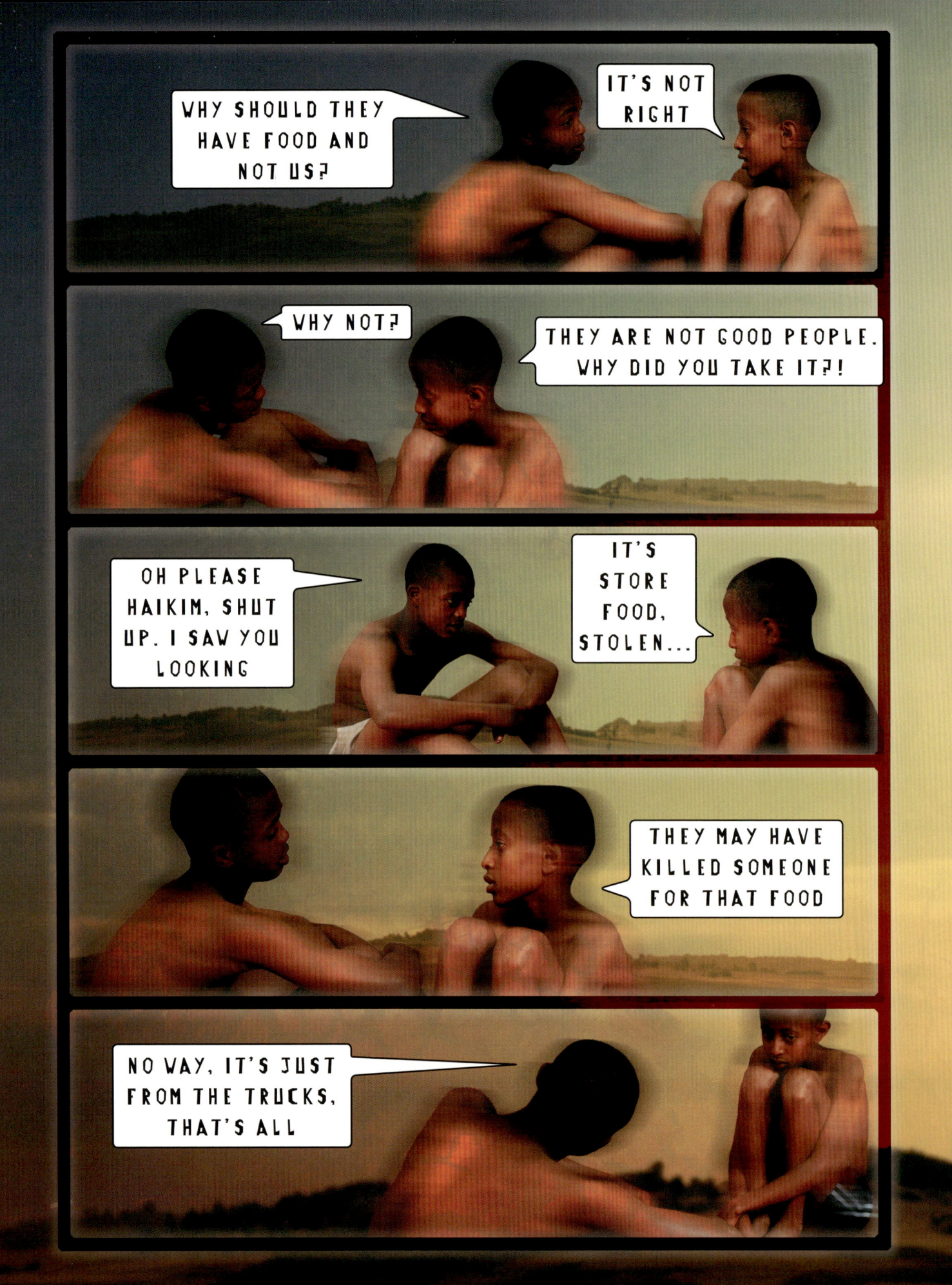

- WHY SHOULD THEY HAVE FOOD AND NOT US?
- IT'S NOT RIGHT
- WHY NOT?
- THEY ARE NOT GOOD PEOPLE. WHY DID YOU TAKE IT?!
- OH PLEASE HAIKIM, SHUT UP. I SAW YOU LOOKING
- IT'S STORE FOOD, STOLEN...
- THEY MAY HAVE KILLED SOMEONE FOR THAT FOOD
- NO WAY, IT'S JUST FROM THE TRUCKS, THAT'S ALL

Did you know the story tree used be down there before the drought?

Let me tell you the story of the girl who went out to cut grass. She saw a place where it was growing luxuriantly, but when she put her foot there she sank at once into the mud. Her friends tried to catch hold of her hands, but she sank deeper into the mud and disappeared. Her friends ran home and called all the people to the quagmire, but she could not be found.

However, on the spot where the girl had sunk a tree began to grow, which got taller and taller until it reached the sky. It was a useful tree under which boys would drive their cattle in the heat of the day. One day two boys climbed up into the tree, calling to their companions that they were going to the world above. They never returned.

The tree was called the Story-tree, it too has now returned to the ground like the girl.

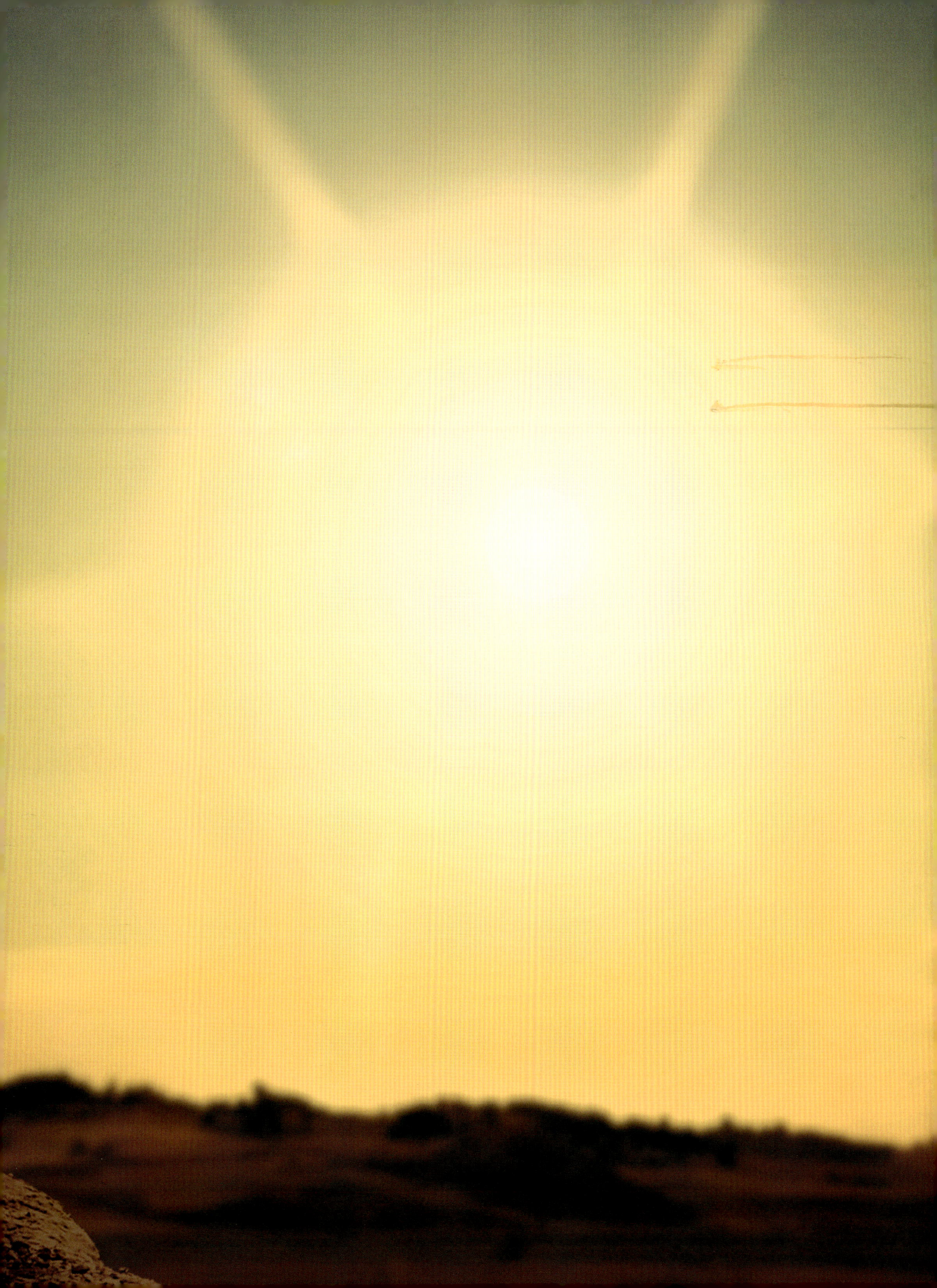

ENOUGH IS ENOUGH

Brothers come in many shapes and sizes. Blood is usually a good indicator of bond, but it is not the only one. Although it is plain to see that Killi and Haikim are not real brothers, they are in spirit. I cannot see other spirits that roam the earth as you may assume, but there is clearly another at work here. Killi's heart is fast to rise, his pride uncontainable. It will nearly take his life on several occasions...

WE NEED FOOD, OUR MOTHER IS SICK
WHAT DO YOU WANT FROM US? I COULD WORK FOR YOU?
PLEASE HELP US SHE IS DYING
WE HAVE NO ONE ELSE THAT CAN HELP

"I HEAR YOU ARE A RUNNER HAIKIM?

IF YOU BEAT ISSI ACROSS THE LINE THEN I'LL GIVE YOU AS MUCH INJERA AND BEANS AS YOU CAN CARRY!

DEAL?"

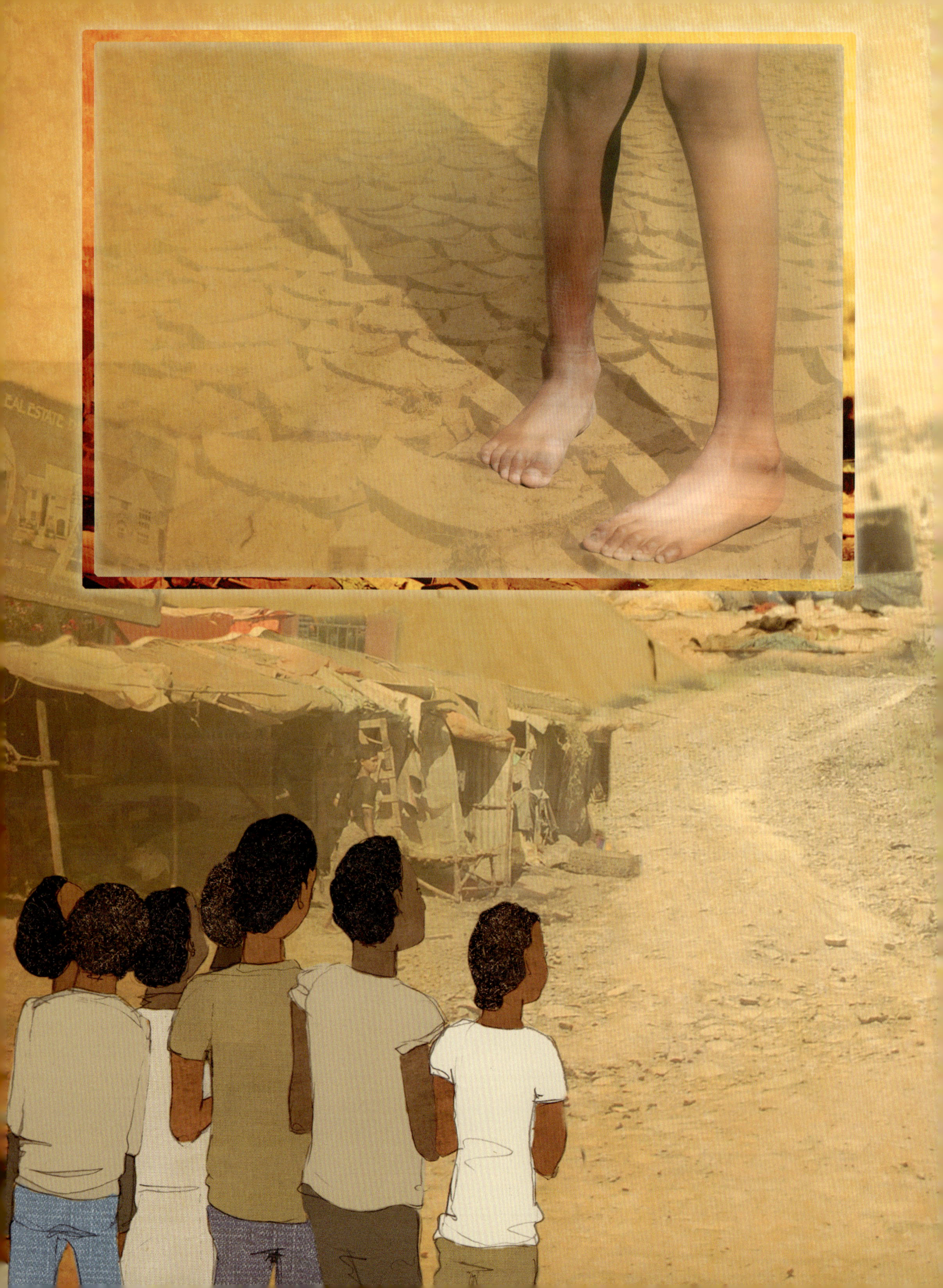

"YOU DON'T LOOK LIKE MUCH OF A RUNNER TO ME BOY..."

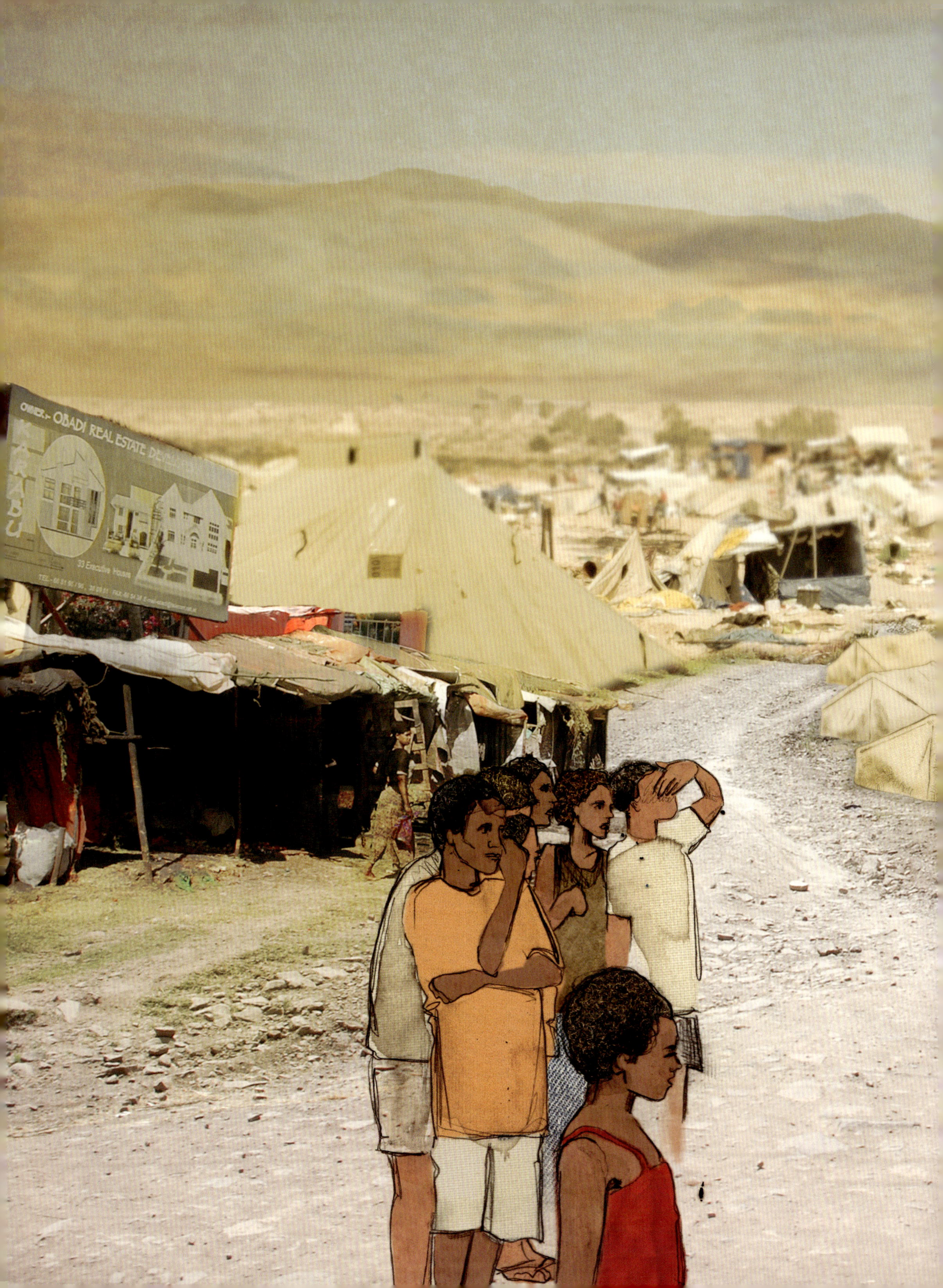
OWNER:- OBADI REAL ESTATE
33 Executive Houses

READY
SET
GO

WHY THE LONG FACE HAIKIM... THE FOOD IS GOOD ISN'T IT?
THIS FOOD IS STOLEN.

CHEGGER YELLEM TAKE TAKE

BLESS YOU

DON'T THANK ME, THANK HAIKIM

THANKYOU HAIKIM...
...OUR CHAMPION

"WHAT WE DID WAS WRONG, I WILL NOT STEAL FOR THEM KILLI"

"WE DO WHAT NEEDS TO BE DONE"

"THAT'S YOUR CHOICE. BUT YOU ARE A FOOL AND A TRAITOR TO OUR FAMILY. TELL ME YOU WON'T GO WITH THEM, BE ONE OF THEM..."

"I ALREADY AM"

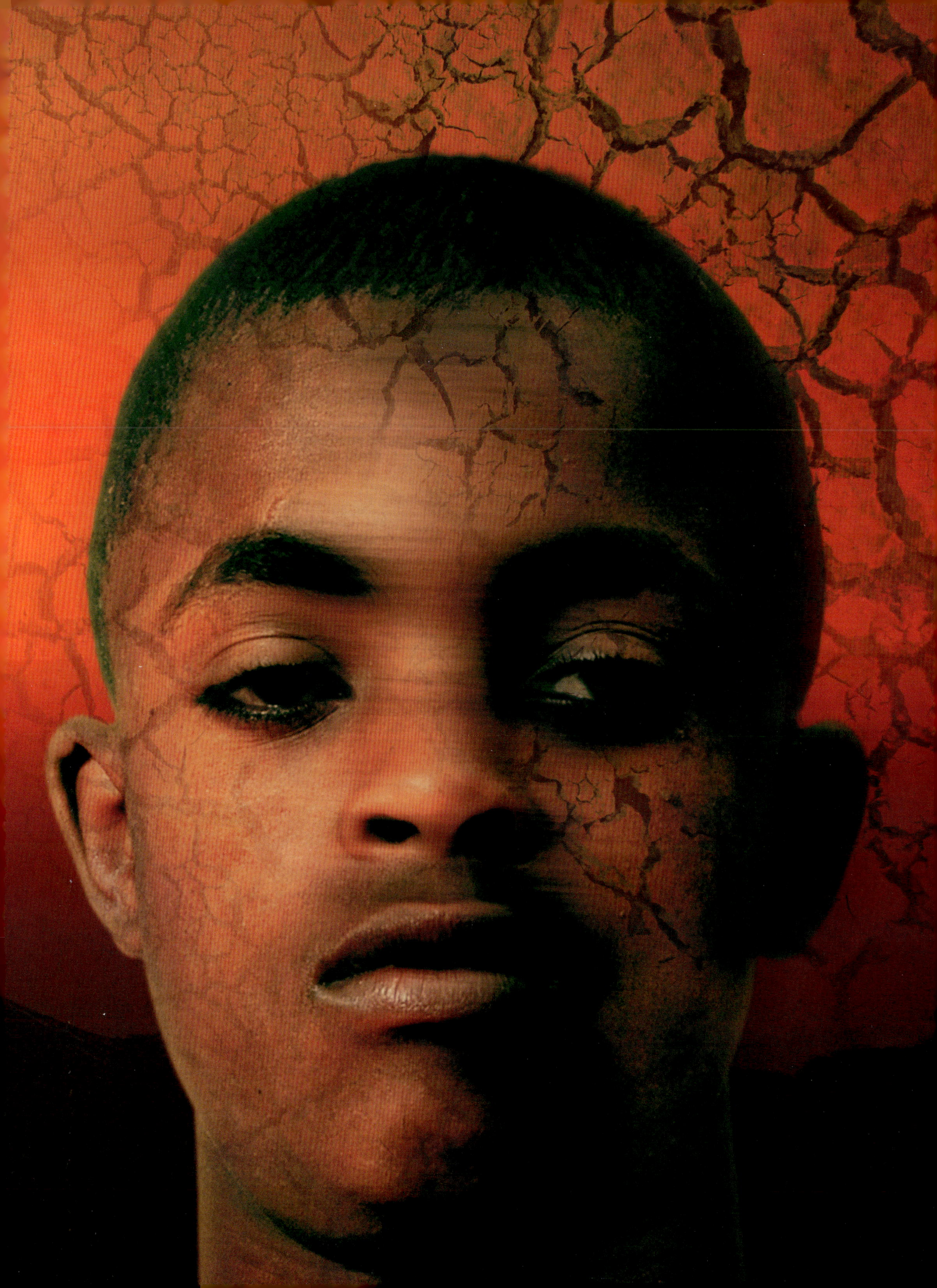

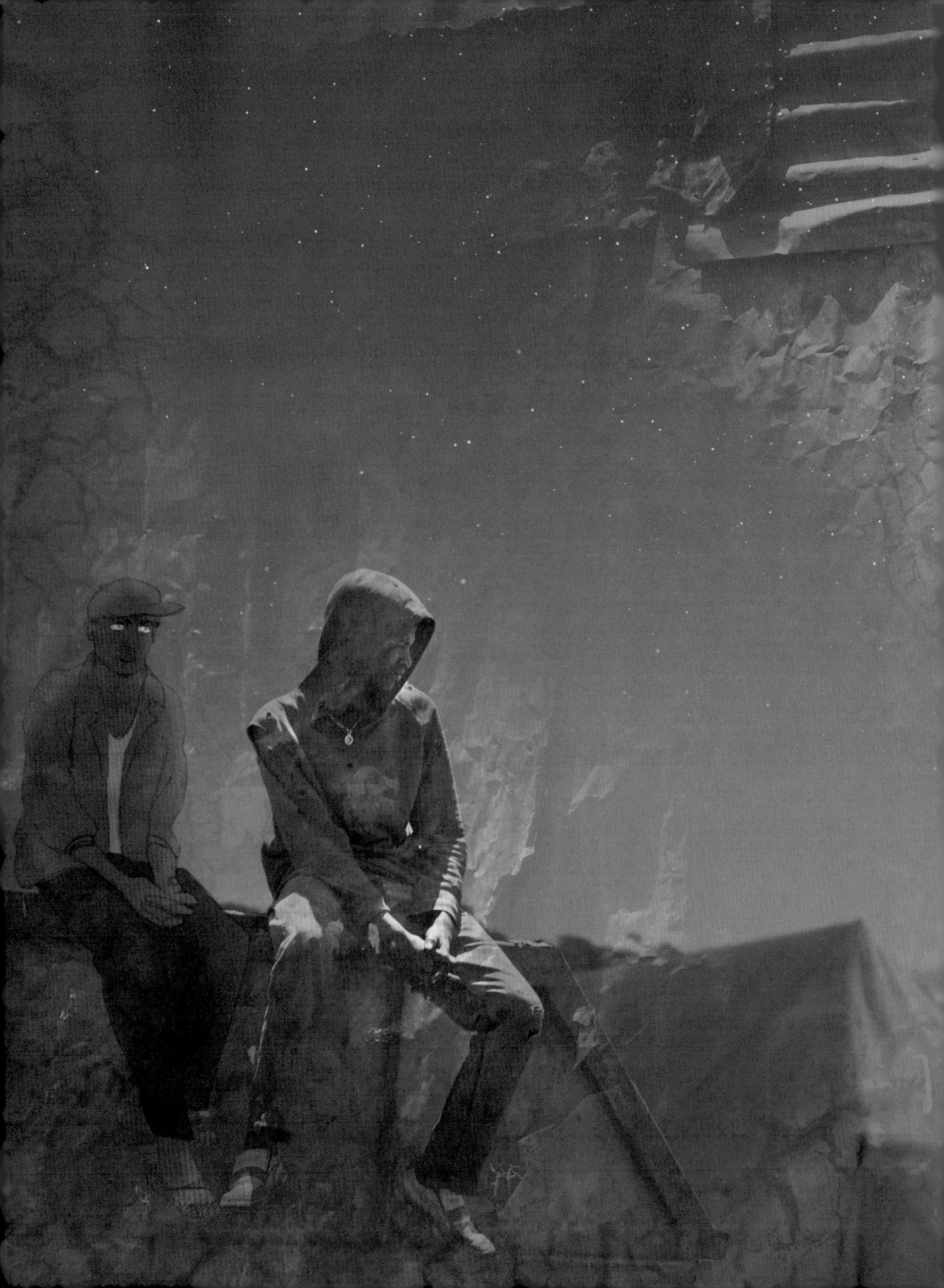

WELCOME KILLI

> EVERY MORNING IN AFRICA A GAZELLE WAKES UP. IT KNOWS IT MUST RUN FASTER THAN THE FASTEST LION OR IT WILL BE KILLED. EVERY MORNING A LION WAKES UP, IT KNOWS IT WILL STARVE TO DEATH IF IT CANNOT CATCH IT'S PREY. IT DOESN'T MATTER IF YOU ARE A LION OR A GAZELLE. WHEN THE SUN COMES UP YOU BETTER START RUNNING

> LIFE IS NOT FAIR. I MUST HELP. I MUST FEED MY FAMILY

Starvation. Illness. Death. What drives us comes from only two places – Hope and Fear. These two are brothers themselves. Two sides of a coin.

HEY YOU! GET BACK HERE THIEF!

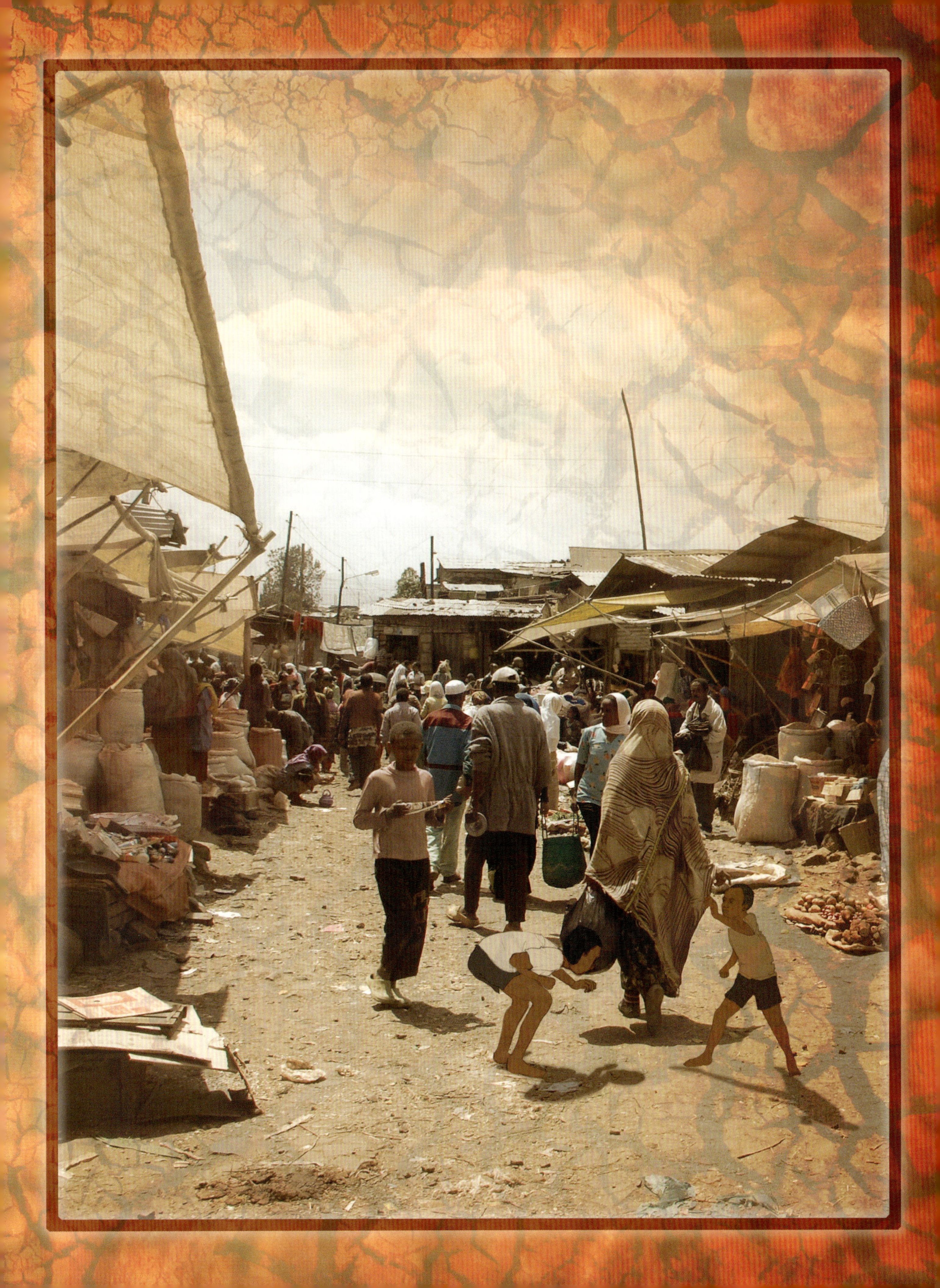

WHEN THE LAST TRUCK STOPS WE JUMP IT... OK?

IT'S A TRAP, RUN!

THEY'RE CLOSE KILLI, KEEP RUNNING

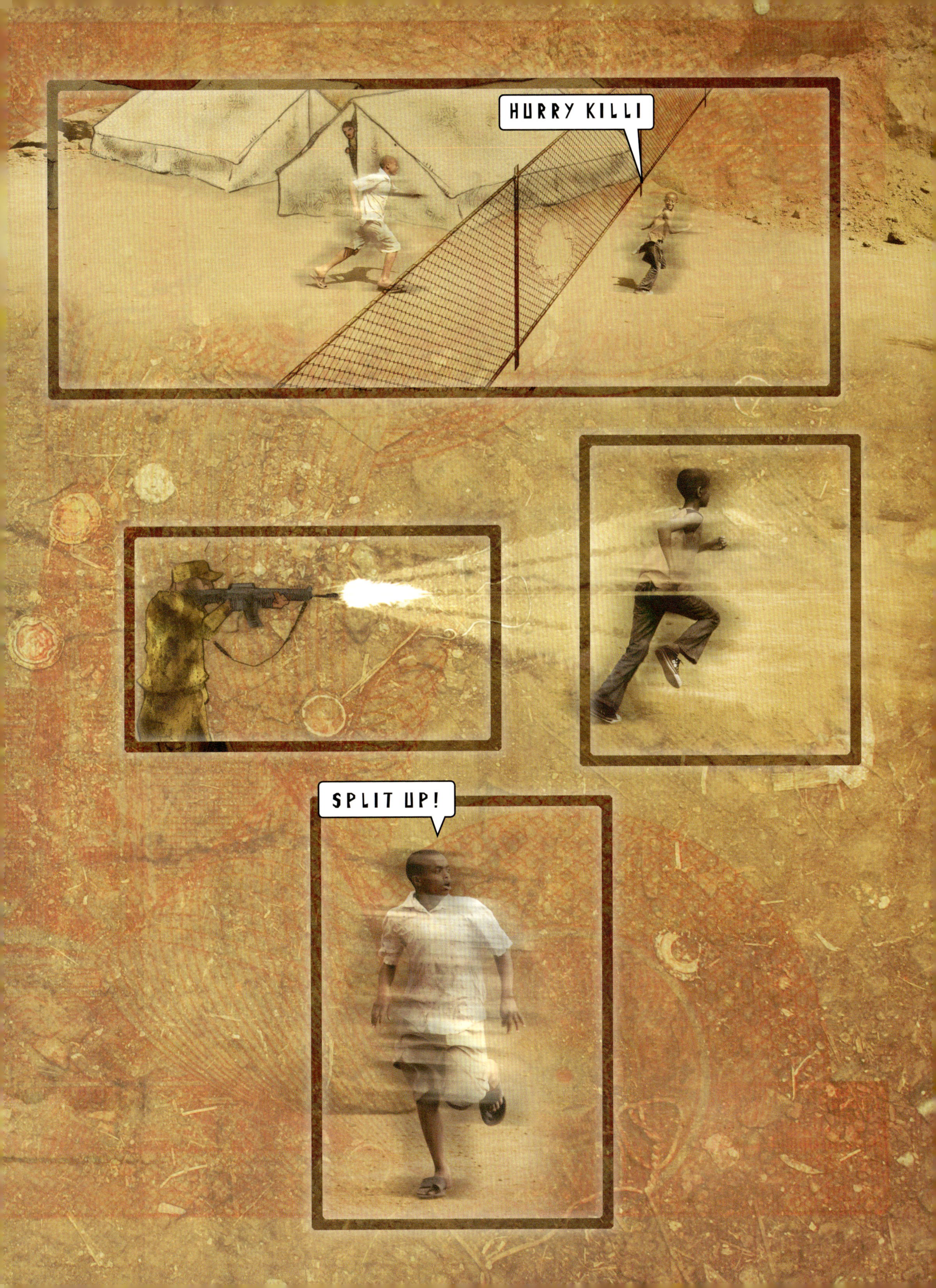
HURRY KILLI
SPLIT UP!

"I'll draw them away. You head for the rocks."

"Run Haikim run!"

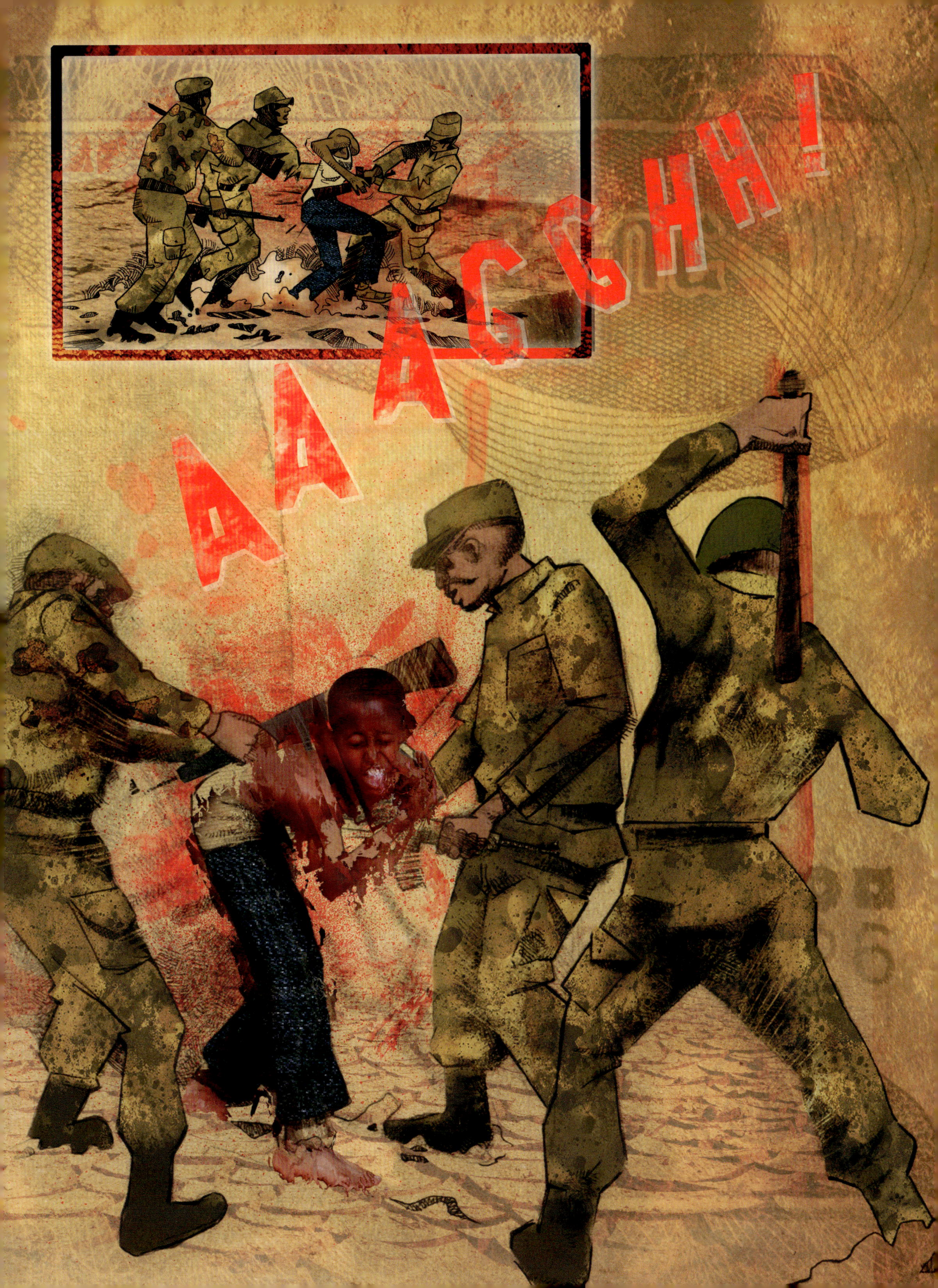
AAAAGGHH!

NOWHERE TO RUN NOW HEY THIEF.

PLEASE!

WHAT'S THIS? LUCKY CHARM? WHERE ARE YOU FROM THIEF?

ASELA

A RUNNER FROM ASELA! WELL THAT'S FITTING!
SEND HIM TO HELL
WE'RE ALREADY IN HELL

THANK GOD YOU'RE ALIVE... THANK GOD.

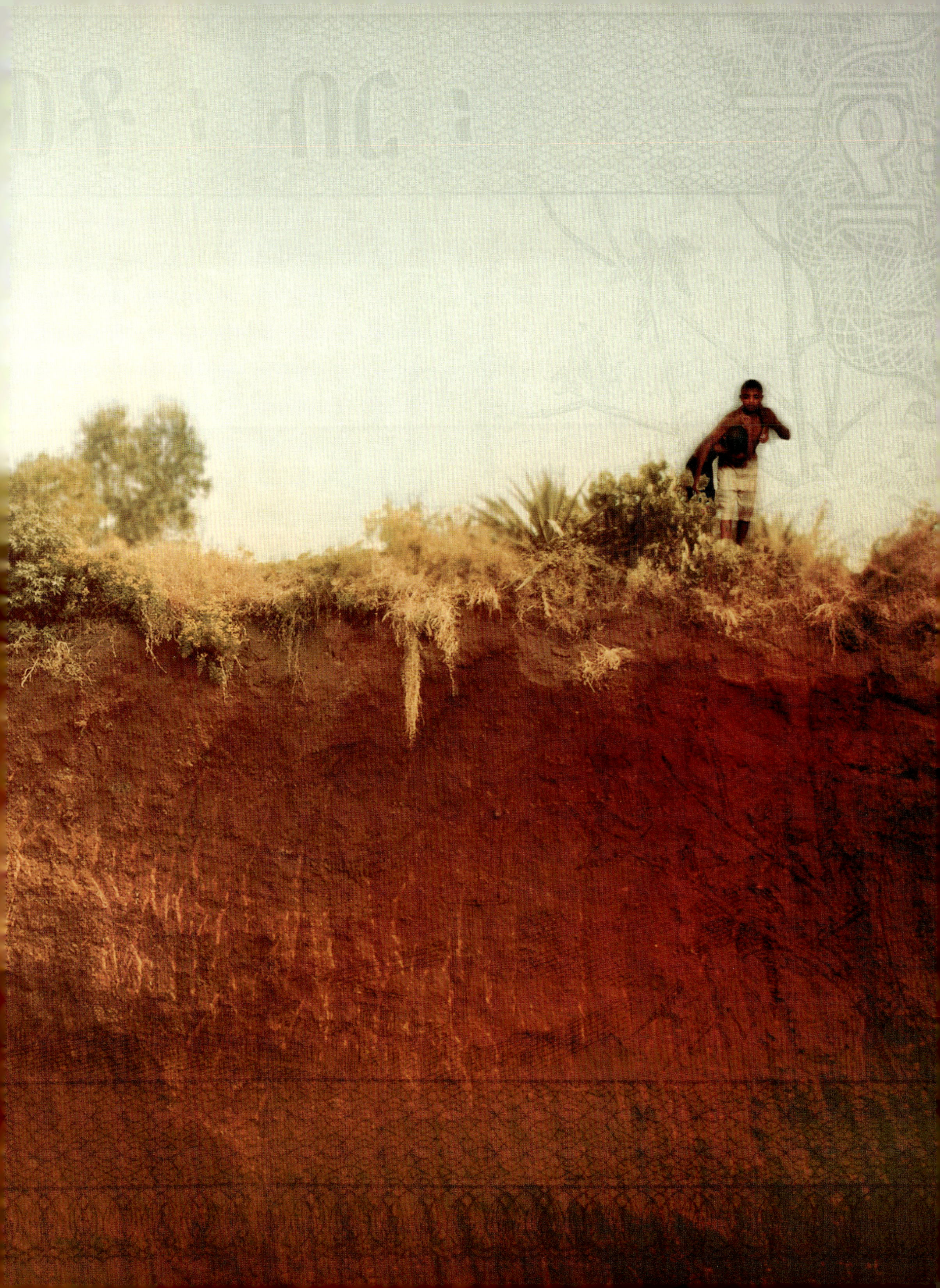

For days Killi nursed him, but even he was surprised by the speed of Haikim's recovery. I did not doubt the fire was still in him. It would not go out until it had done what it had set out to do.

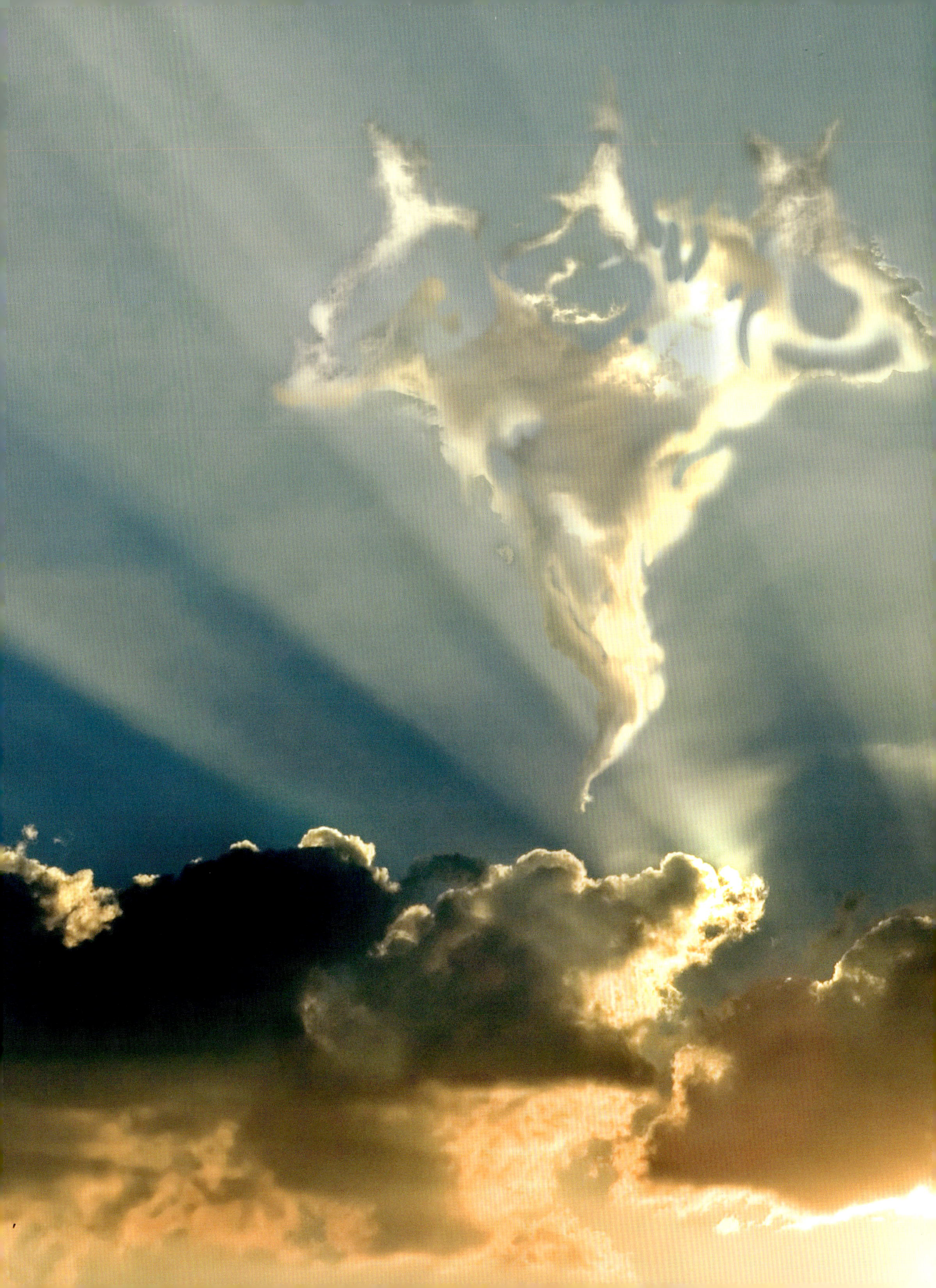

The Shebelle was their escape route, 12 days to the North East they walked, stealing food and marching through the night. Killi knew the river would lead them to the Sea eventually.

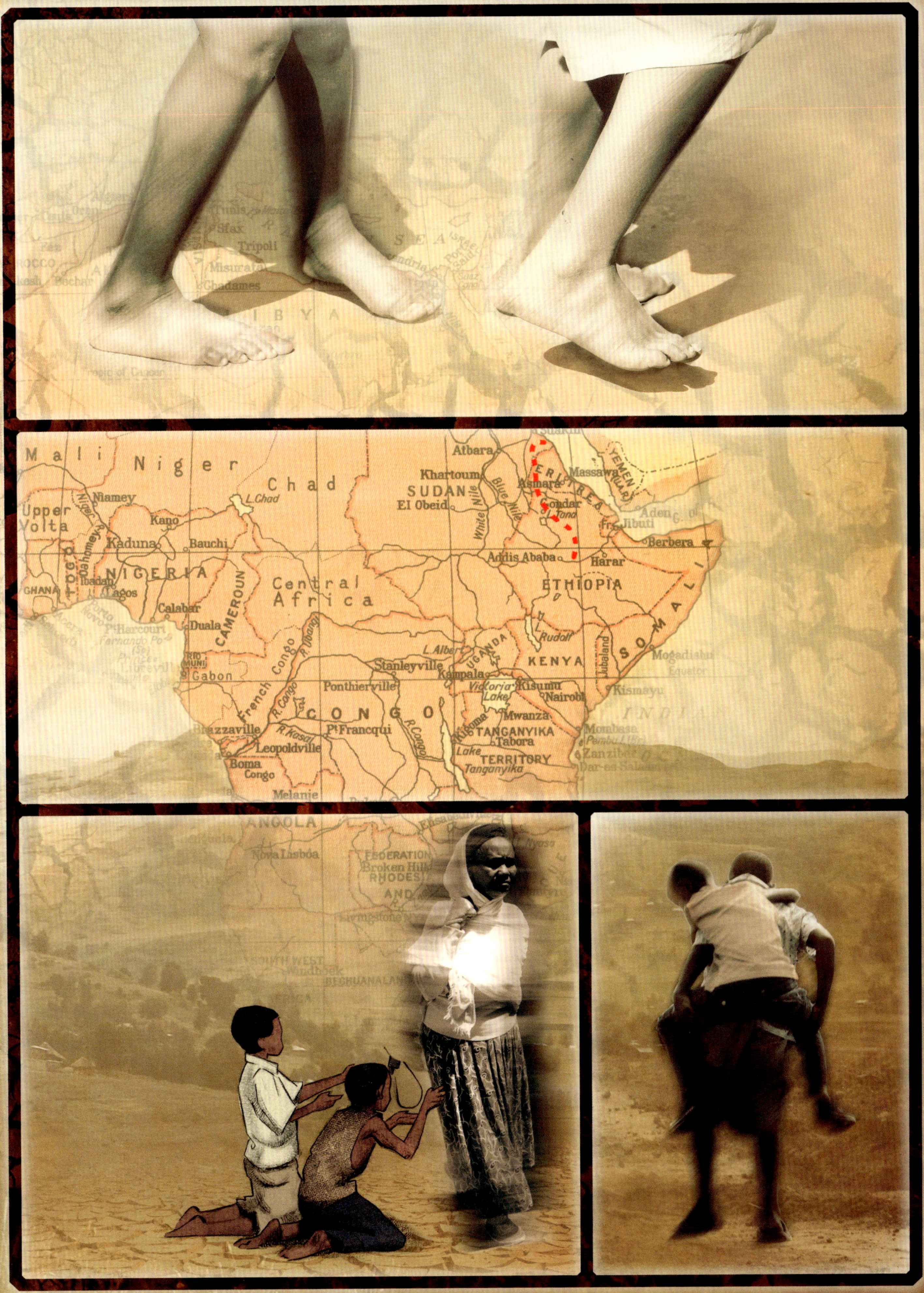
Mali
Niger
Chad
L. Chad
Niamey
Upper Volta
Kano
Kaduna
Bauchi
NIGERIA
Ibadan
Lagos
GHANA
Togo
Dahomey
Calabar
Duala
CAMEROUN
Central Africa
Gabon
French Congo
Brazzaville
Leopoldville
Boma
Congo
CONGO
Ponthierville
Stanleyville
P^t Francqui
Atbara
Khartoum
SUDAN
El Obeid
White Nile
Blue Nile
ERITREA
Asmara
Gondar
Massawa
YEMEN
Aden
Jibuti
Berbera
Harar
Addis Ababa
ETHIOPIA
SOMALIA
Rudolf
KENYA
Kampala
UGANDA
L. Albert
Victoria Lake
Kisumu
Nairobi
Kismayu
Mogadishu
Mwanza
TANGANYIKA
Tabora
TERRITORY
Lake Tanganyika
Mombasa
Zanzibar
Melanje
ANGOLA
Nova Lisboa
FEDERATION
Broken Hill
RHODESIA
Tripoli
Misurata
Ghadames
Sfax
LIBYA

Atlantic Ocean

Bay of Biscay

FRANCE

SWITZERLAND
Bern
MONACO
ANDORRA
Andorra

PORTUGAL
Lisbon

Balearic

Costa Del Sol

Mediterranean

Strait of Gibraltar

Algiers

Rabat

MOROCCO

TUNIS

ALGERIA

They grew up running. From street gangs in Sudan to sweat shops in Egypt. Traded in child slavery, only escaping to hawk fake trainers on dirty streets. Ten years blurred by misery as they beg, steal and borrow across the ports and beaches of Africa and finally into Europe. Raids, gangs, beatings, drugs, abuse and the old enemy starvation follow their shadows. As men they have grown into their role as Lookie Lookie men; scratching a living selling stolen goods to tourists, running from the law and watching each others back. Living between the cracks of the modern world.

1 Hour to race...

WHY DO THEY CALL YOU LOOKIE?

"IT'S A LONG STORY... MAYBE LATER."

Costa Del Sol

Who are you? What are you made of? What could you be? If you know the answers to such questions you have most likely experienced defeat many times. For it is only when the spirit is tested that true character is revealed.

The streets claim many of those that visit. No obvious place to find redemption and re-birth but for Haikim it was ideal.

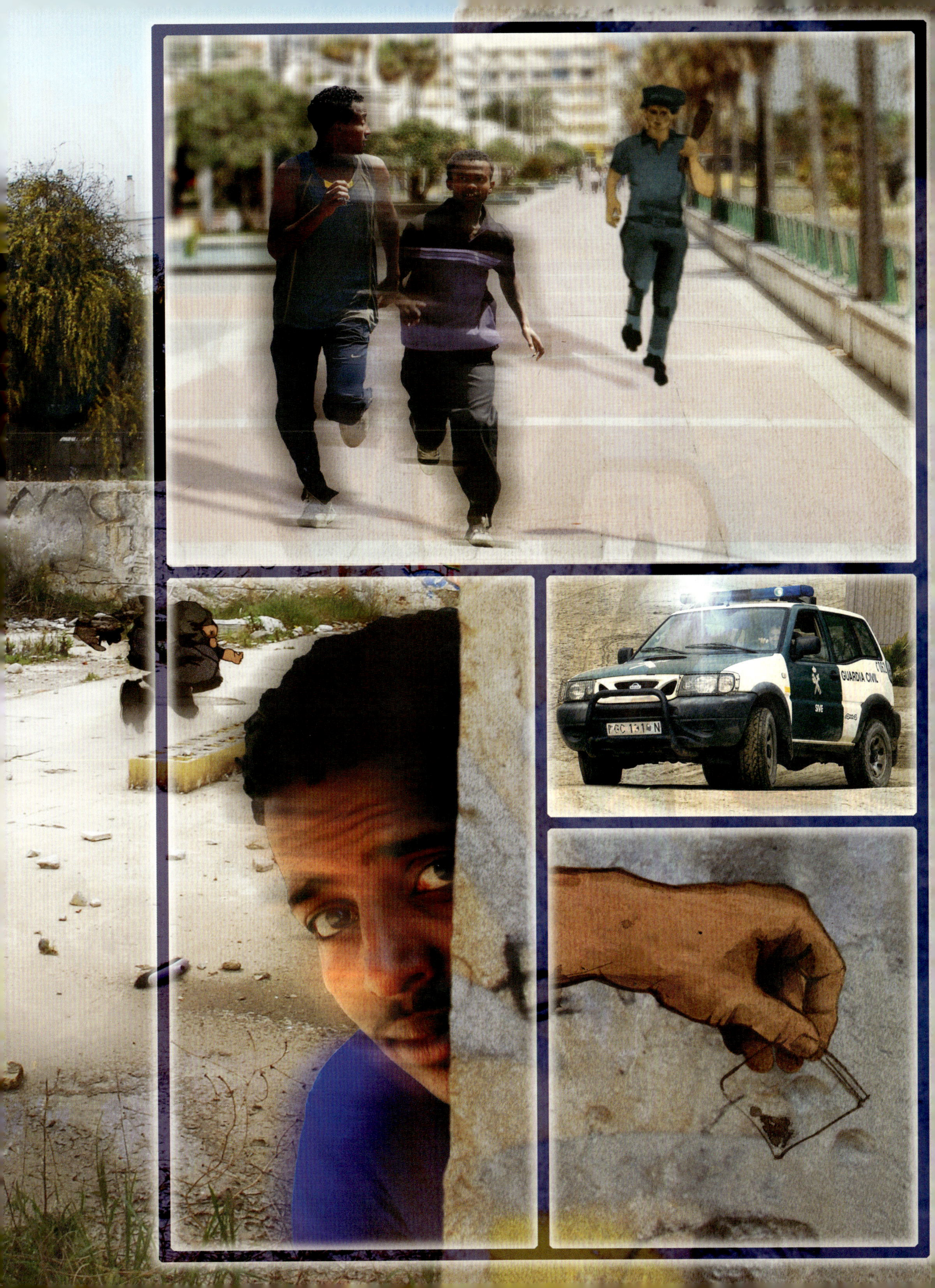
GUARDIA CIVIL

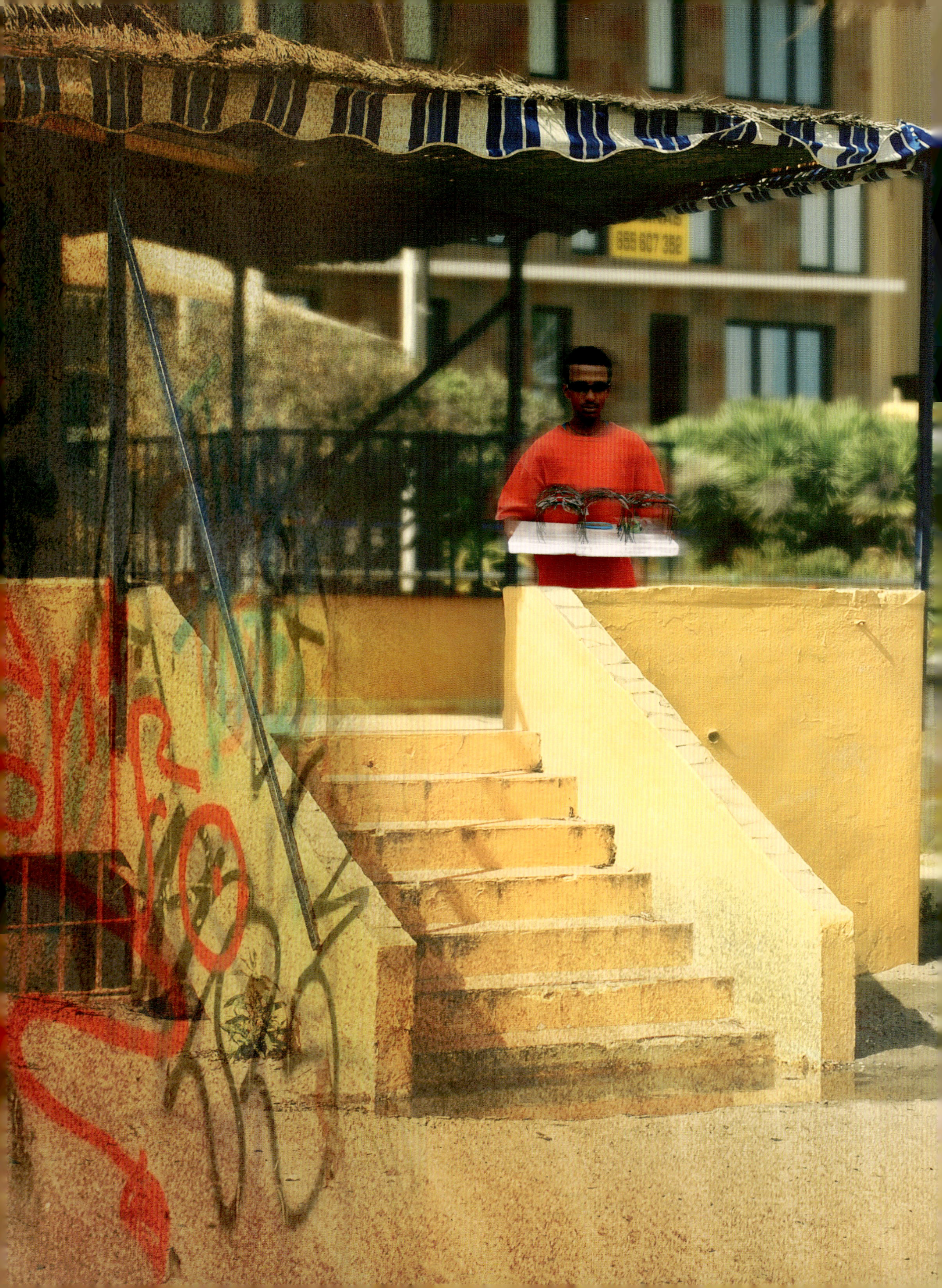

You may wonder how I know of other spirits if I cannot see them. Sometimes they strike without warning with a force not even I can match.

> It's trash
>
> Natalie
>
> What's your name?
>
> I'm Haikim

I WANT TO STAY WITH YOU...

THAT'S NOT POSSIBLE NATALIE, NOT YET

"I don't care about possible, I care about you. I love you Haikim"

We have all witnessed this before. A flame easily ignited can also be put out by the touch of another. For Haikim it was part of his journey, his training. Suddenly part of something. Open to a broader view of life.

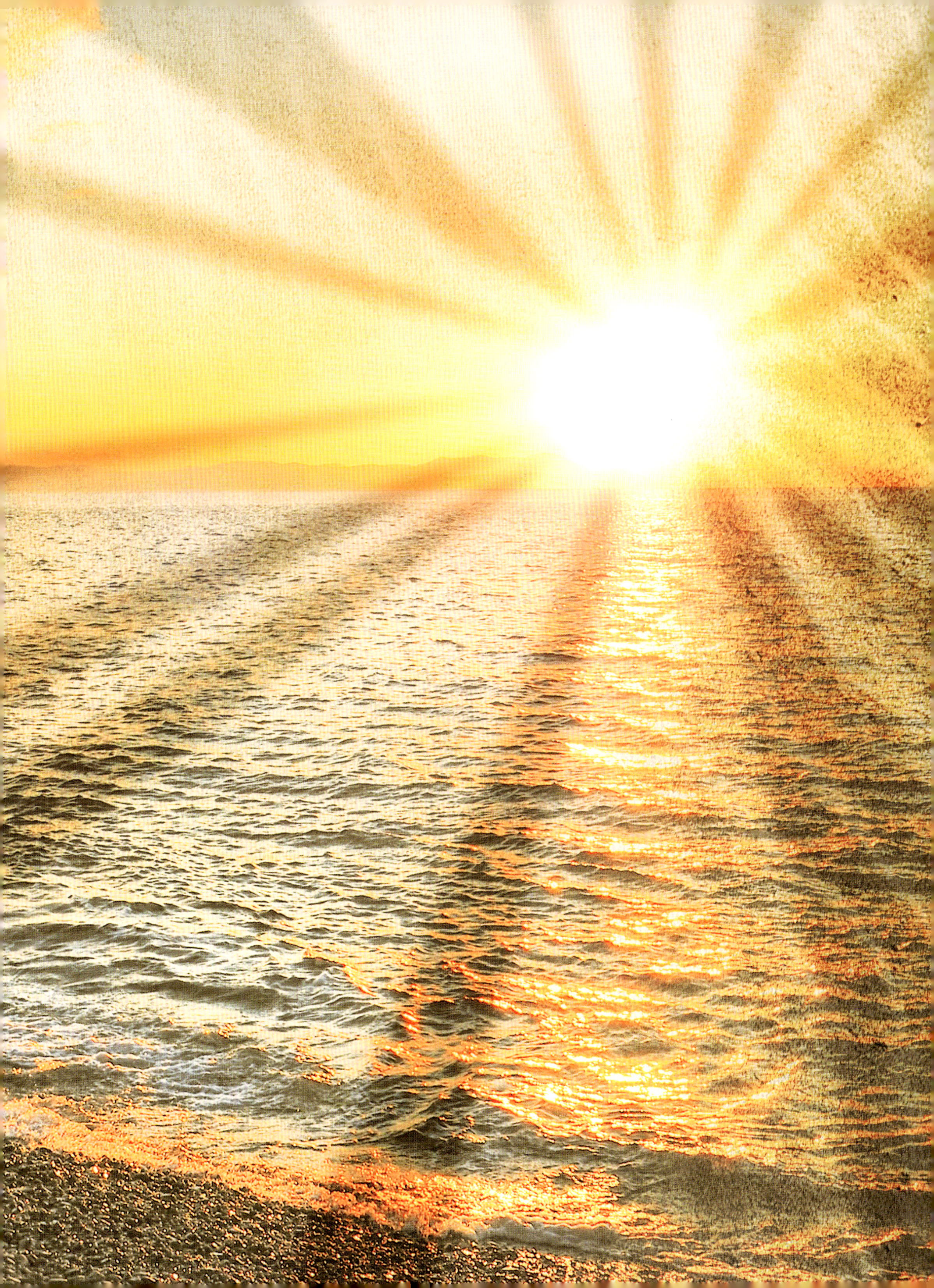

But love is not for sprinters.

"So this is where you have been all holidays..."

"Father... this is Haikim."

TELL ME, WHERE ARE YOU FROM HAIKIM? SIERRA LEONE? GAMBIA? DO YOU HAVE A HOME EVEN?

PLEASE LET HER GO.

IT'S HER CHOICE

SHE'S 22. SHE'S BEEN TRAINING HER WHOLE LIFE AS A GYMNAST. THIS YEAR WILL BE HER LAST CHANCE AT A MEDAL.

PLEASE UNDERSTAND IT'S NOTHING TO DO WITH... IT'S JUST... WELL SHE IS ONLY MONTHS AWAY FROM HER DREAM.

I WILL COME BACK, MAYBE NEXT MONTH?

YOU DID WHAT? I CAN'T BELIEVE HE SAID THAT TO YOU!

LEAVE IT KILLI

LEAVE IT? YOU LEFT HER... HOW COULD YOU?

I'M ASHAMED TO CALL YOU MY BROTHER. ALL MY LIFE I PROTECTED YOU... IF YOU DON'T FIGHT FOR HER YOU DON'T DESERVE HER

YOU'RE NOT EVEN MY REAL BROTHER

NO MORE HAIKIM, NO MORE. I WILL NOT PROTECT YOU AGAIN

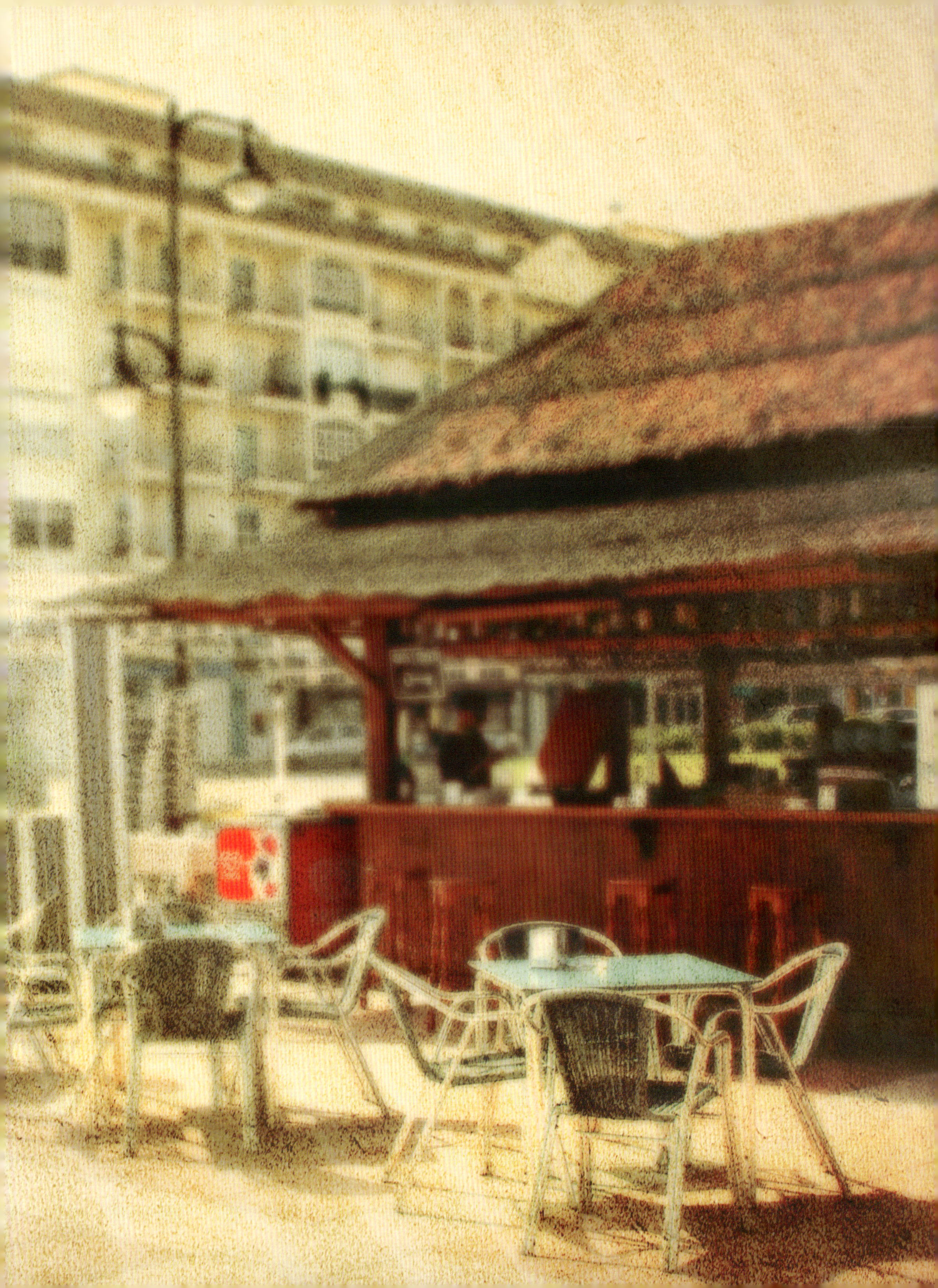

Dark shadows swirl when one is lost. It can go on for a lifetime unless you can pull back. Seeing Natalie that day in the bar on television competing at some championships started a fire.

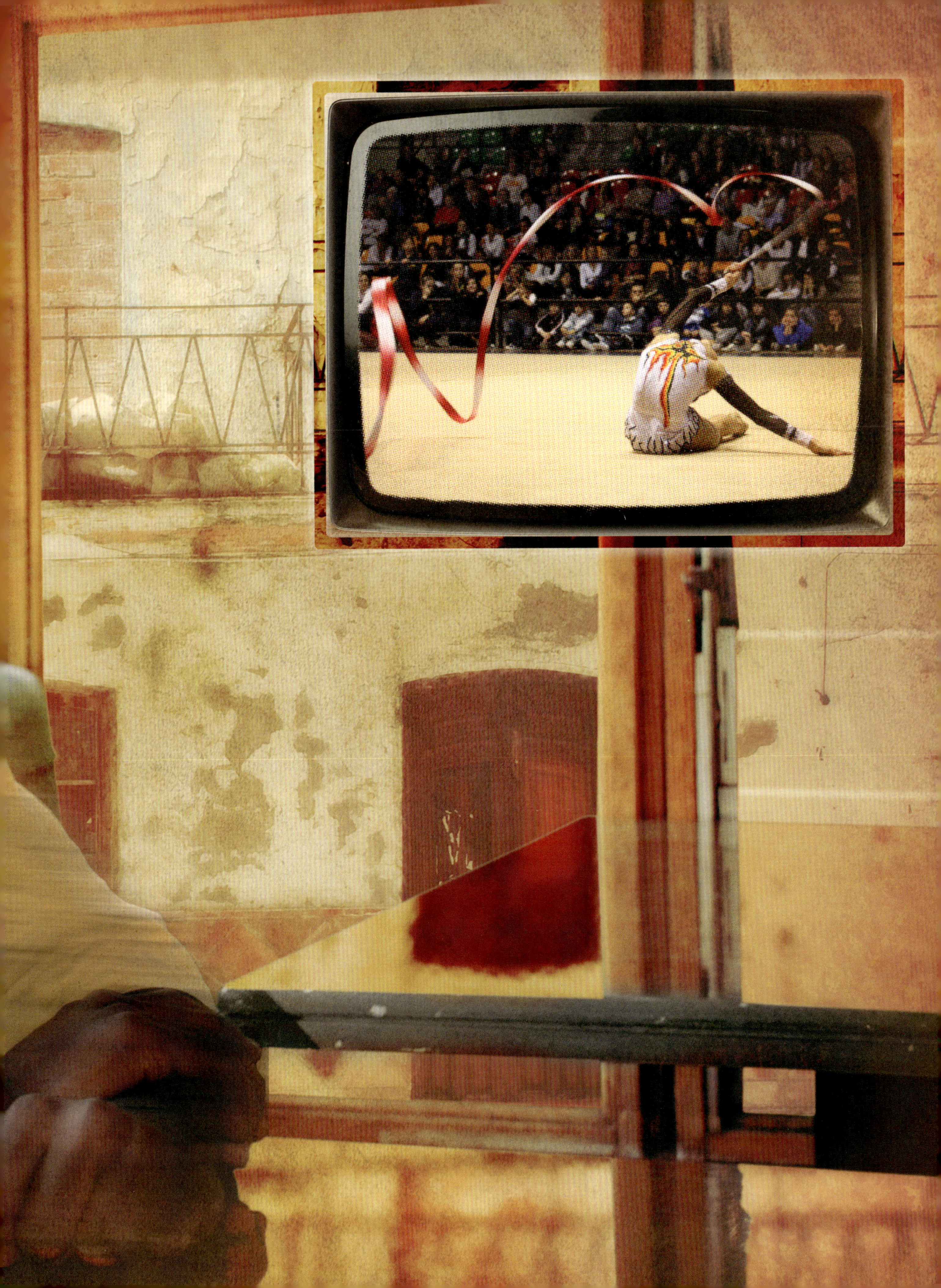

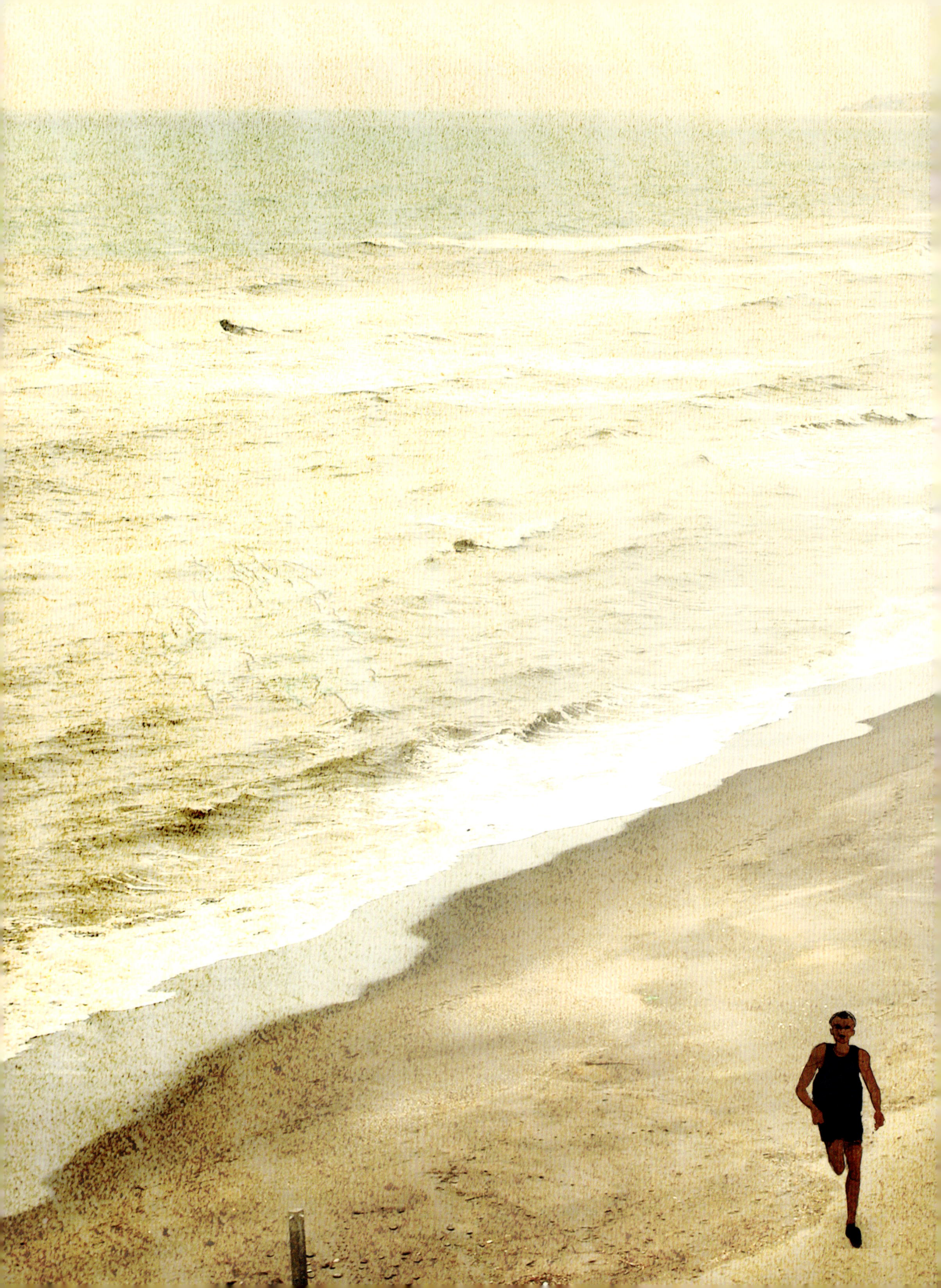

It's interesting to watch the colours change. Red can sometimes appear blue even azure, but over time it burns away and returns with greater ferocity. To me he burns brighter than the sun. Running his heart out. Always running.

BBC pre-race interview

Everyone is talking about the new Ethiopian that runs barefoot...

Can you tell us why you choose not to wear trainers?

How do you respond to the allegations of drug taking to explain your performances?

Do you really expect people to believe this is possible from an athlete from the street? One that has been running for only a year?

IT'S JUST...

ME?

A YEAR? I'VE BEEN RUNNING ALL MY LIFE...

Costa Del Sol
LOOKIE, LOOKIE...
NIKE, ADIDAS, PUMA
HELLO MY FRIEND

> HOW MUCH FOR THESE?

> THIRTY EUROS

> FOR FAKES – YOU MUST BE JOKING...

> I'LL GIVE YOU 10 EUROS NO MORE...

IS THIS MAN ANNOYING YOU SIR?
I'M JUST SELLING TRAINERS
WELL HE'S CERTAINLY A THIEF AT THESE PRICES
ENOUGH OF THIS

CLEAR THIS AREA NOW STREET RAT. THE 10 K IS ABOUT TO START. MAYBE IF YOU BOTHERED TO RUN IN THEM YOU'D KNOW HOW BAD THESE FAKES ARE
FORGET HIM HAIKIM, HE'S NOT WORTH THE TROUBLE
NO. I WILL JOIN THE RACE AND BEAT HIM FAIR AND SQUARE
COME BACK HAIKIM YOU IDIOT
MEET ME AT THE FINISH LINE!

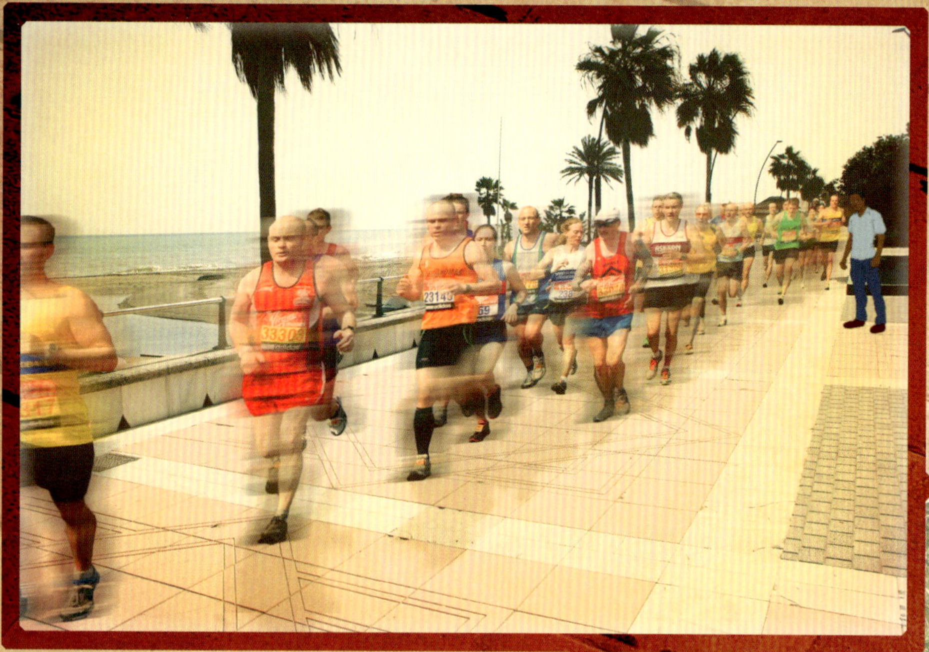

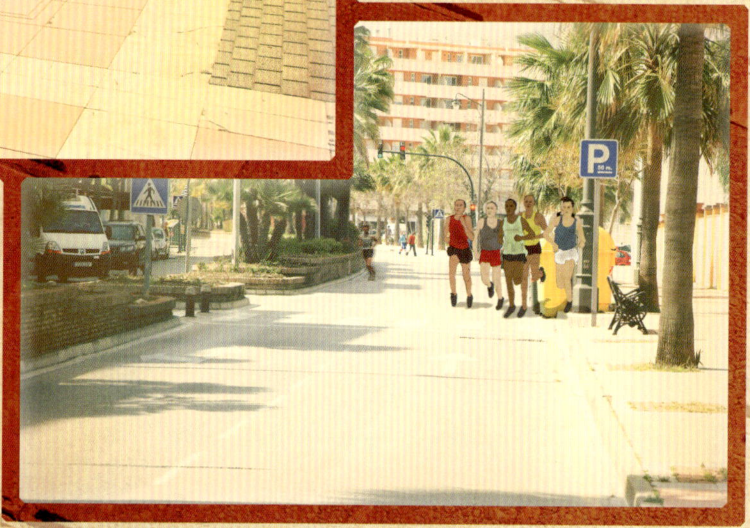
P

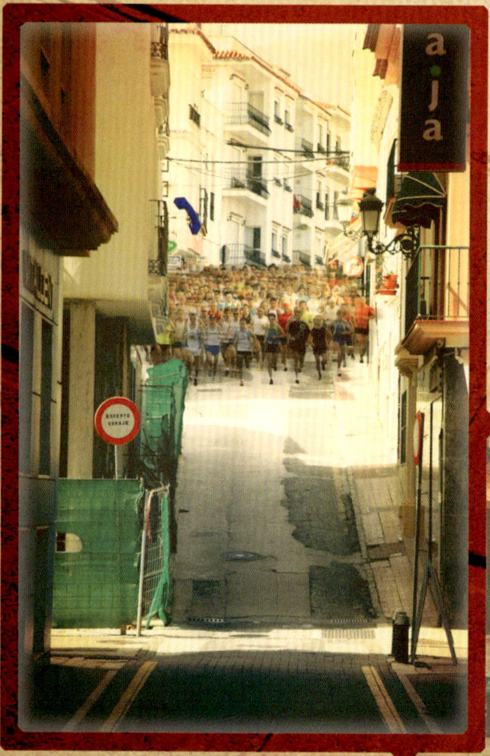
aja

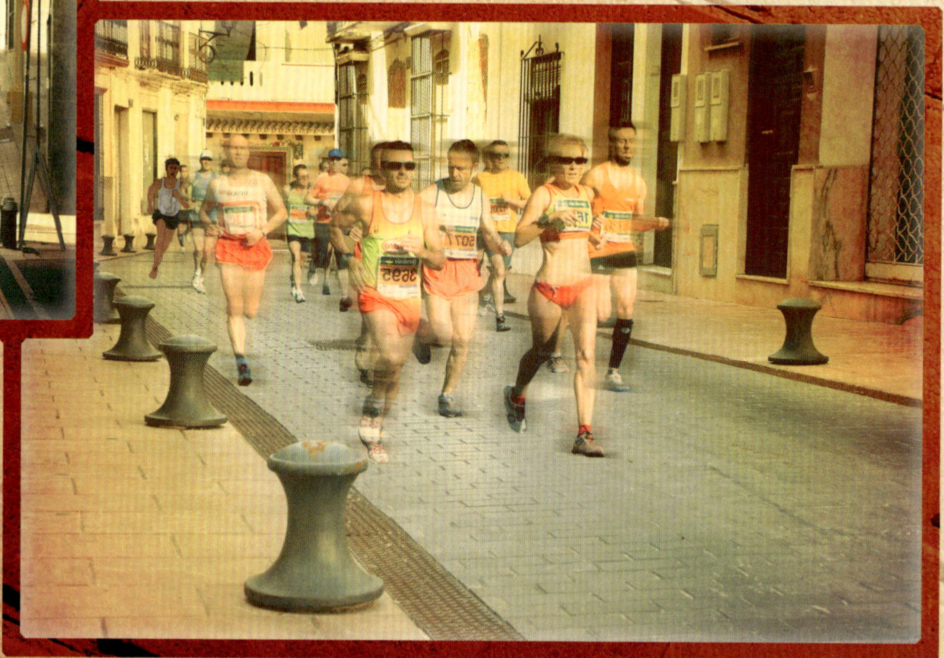

"YOU'RE RIGHT. THOSE TRAINERS ARE RUBBISH..."

"CHAMPION! YOU'RE A CRAZY MAN HAIKIM!"

Costa Del Sol

The stories of his youth came back to him. He found the treasure they helped him bury.

27:07

27:33

27:52

28:04

28:04

28:22

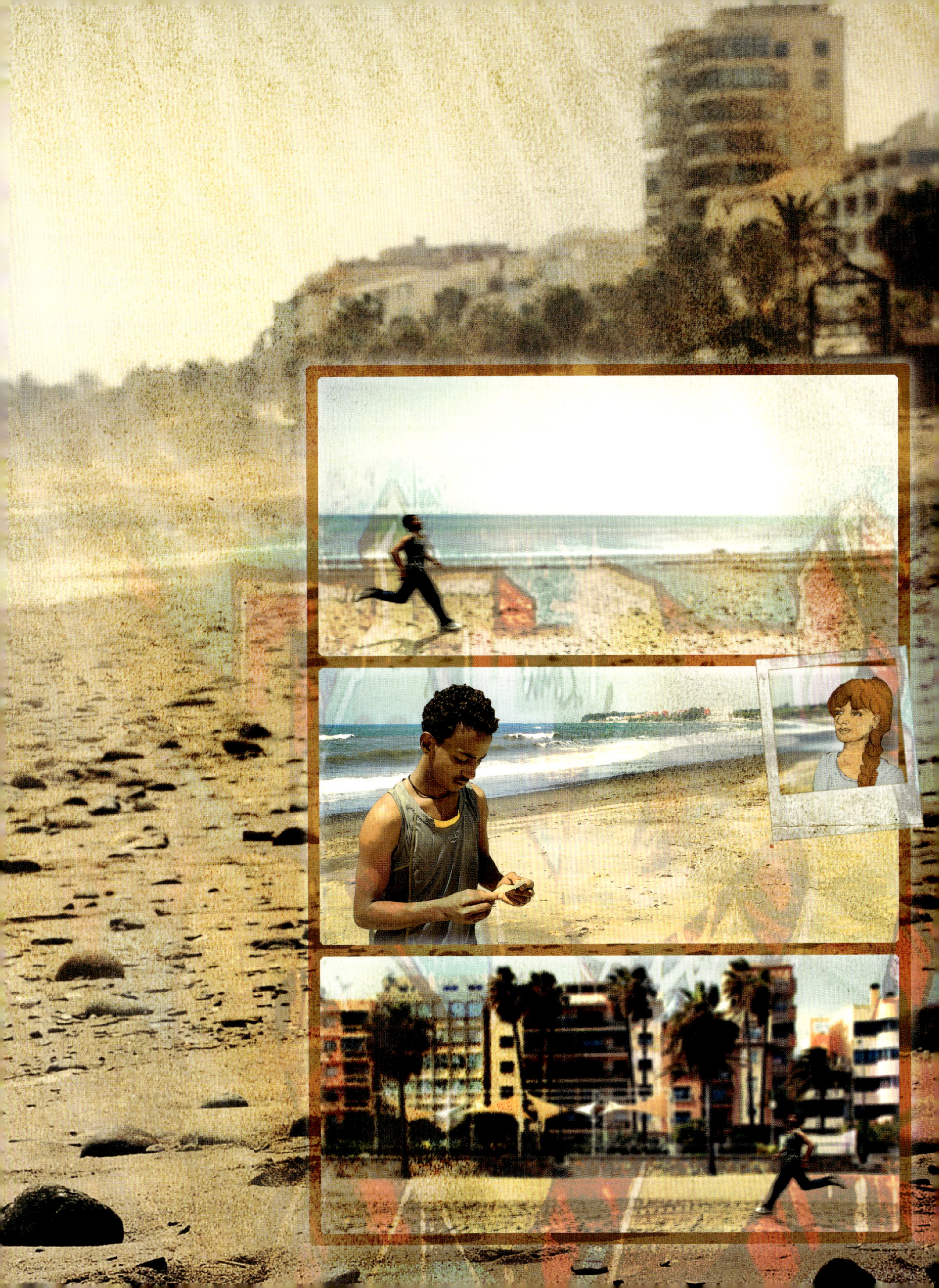

WHERE HAVE YOU BEEN?

NOWHERE

YOU DISAPPEARED FOR A MONTH

DO YOU STILL MISS HER?

I THOUGHT SO...

KYAT TELLS ME YOU'RE RUNNING AGAIN. WHAT TIME YOU MAKE?

27:00 - 28:00

TEN THOUSAND METRES?

SO IT'S TRUE? BEKELE RUNS 26:17

DO YOU NOT SEE WHAT LIFE IS TELLING YOU HAIKIM?

THAT'S A CHAMPIONSHIP FINISHING TIME... THIS IS FOR YOU

"WHERE DID YOU GET THE MONEY FOR THIS KILLI?"

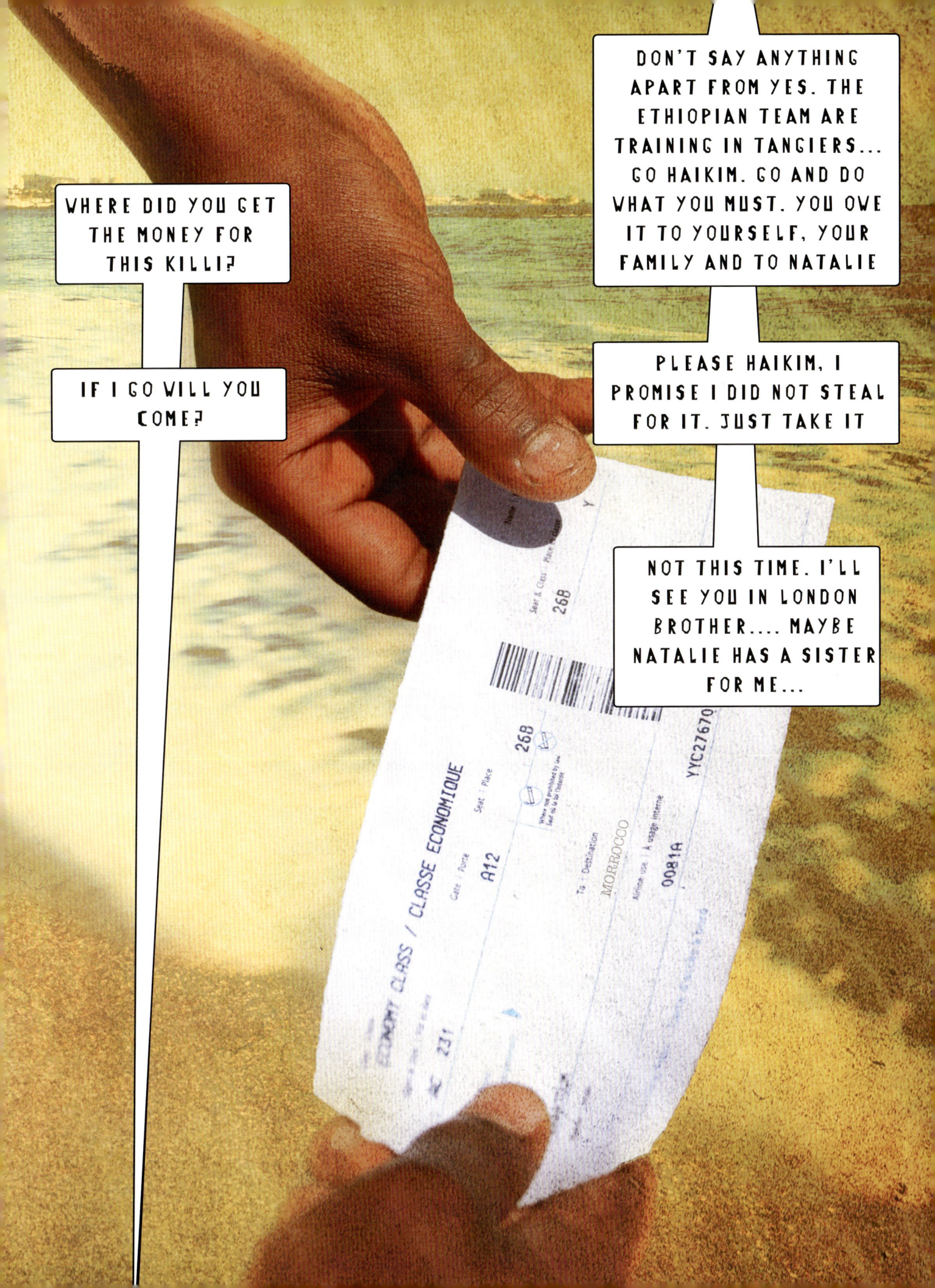

"DON'T SAY ANYTHING APART FROM YES. THE ETHIOPIAN TEAM ARE TRAINING IN TANGIERS... GO HAIKIM. GO AND DO WHAT YOU MUST. YOU OWE IT TO YOURSELF, YOUR FAMILY AND TO NATALIE"

"IF I GO WILL YOU COME?"

"PLEASE HAIKIM, I PROMISE I DID NOT STEAL FOR IT. JUST TAKE IT"

"NOT THIS TIME. I'LL SEE YOU IN LONDON BROTHER.... MAYBE NATALIE HAS A SISTER FOR ME..."

20 Minutes to race

"BEKELE?"

"SO YOU'RE THE 'BAREFOOT RUNNER' NOW"

"ARE YOU READY HAIKIM?"

I THINK SO
I THINK YOU ARE READY. YOU ALWAYS WERE. LIFE HAS PREPARED YOU FOR THIS MOMENT.

Tangiers

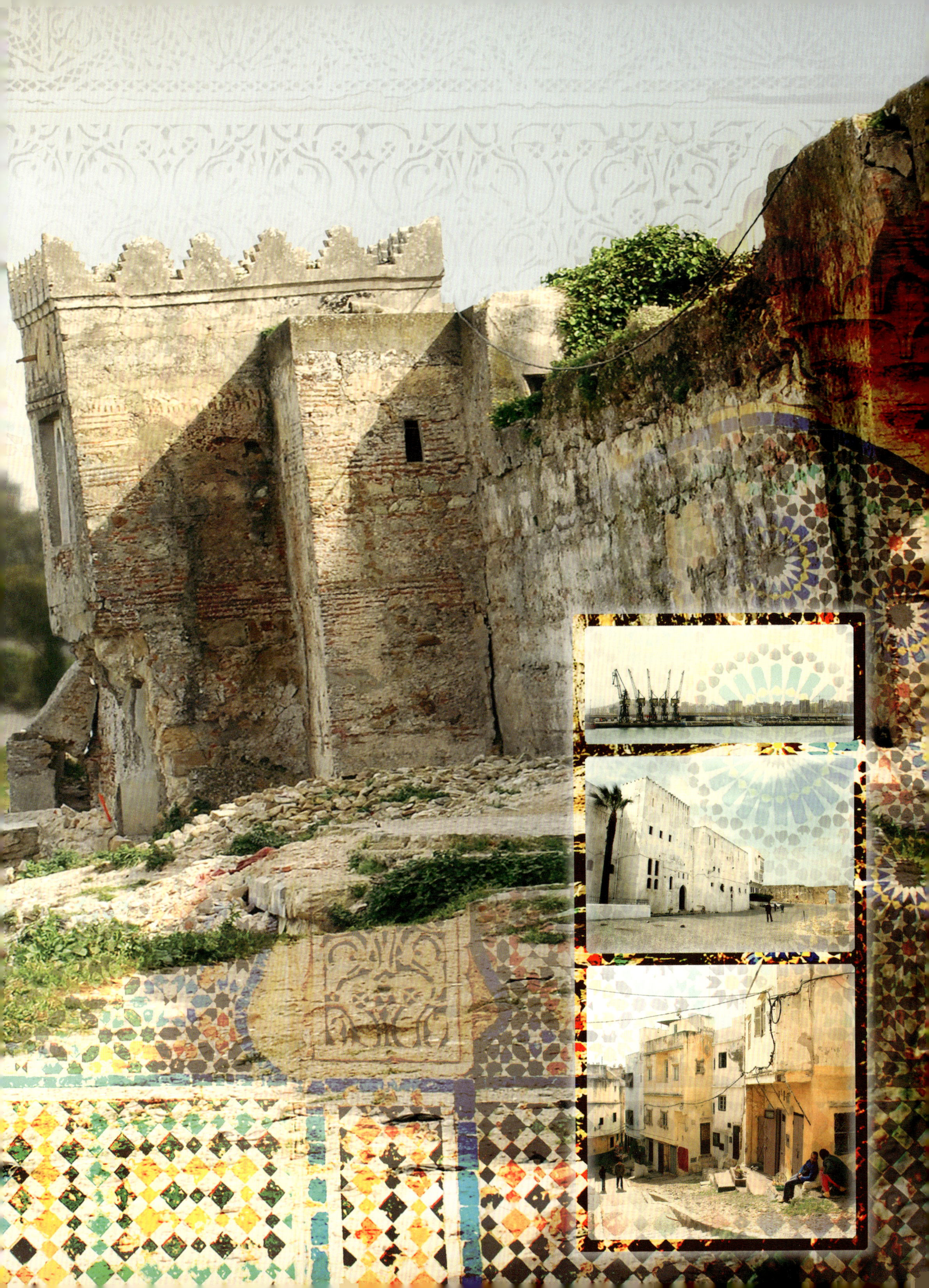

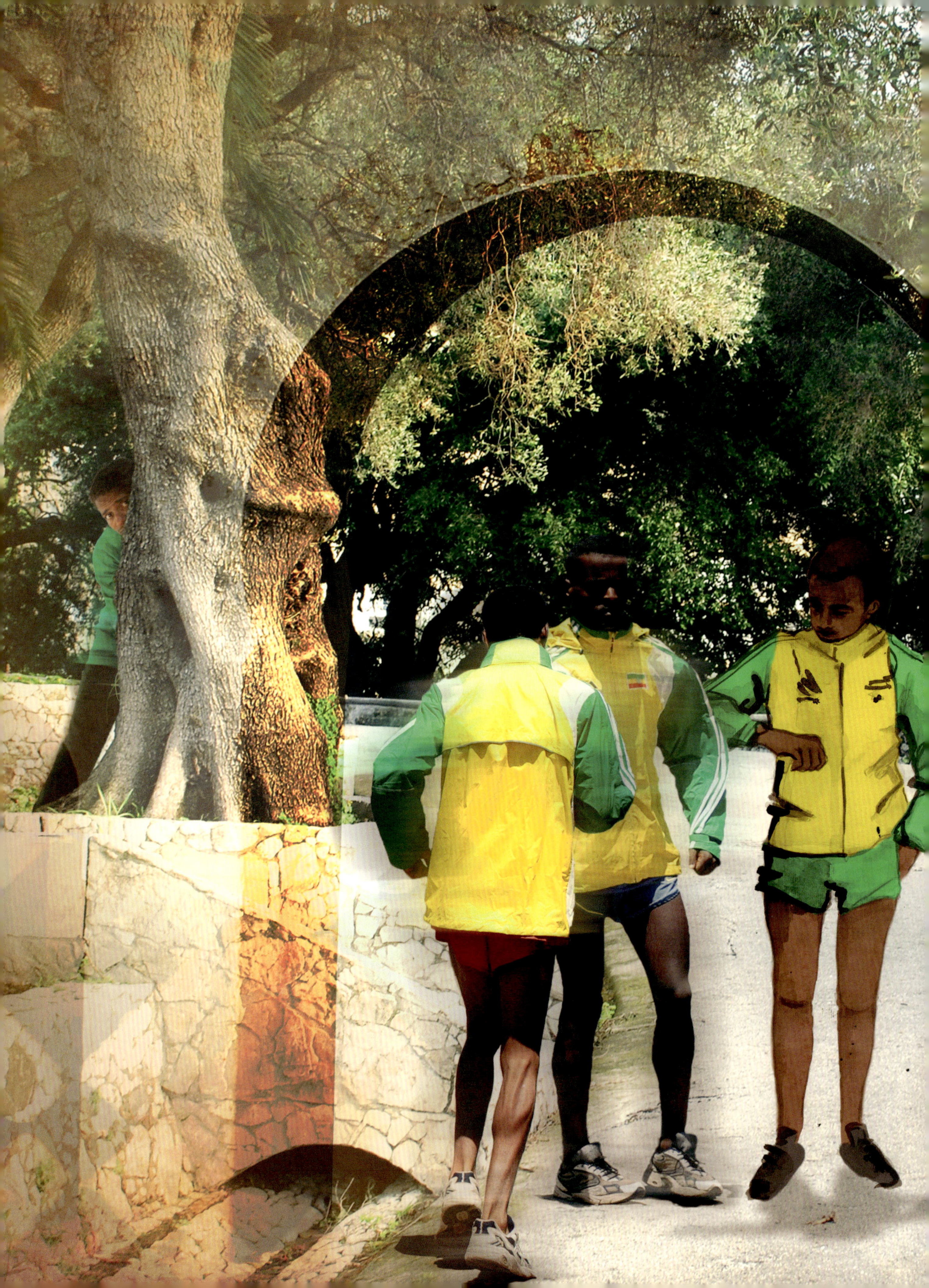

They are glorious together. Like watching the colours of fire at play. Flames from higher ground have a denser feel. They lighten as they fall to sea level. The Rift Valley is perfect and these runners are testimony to it.

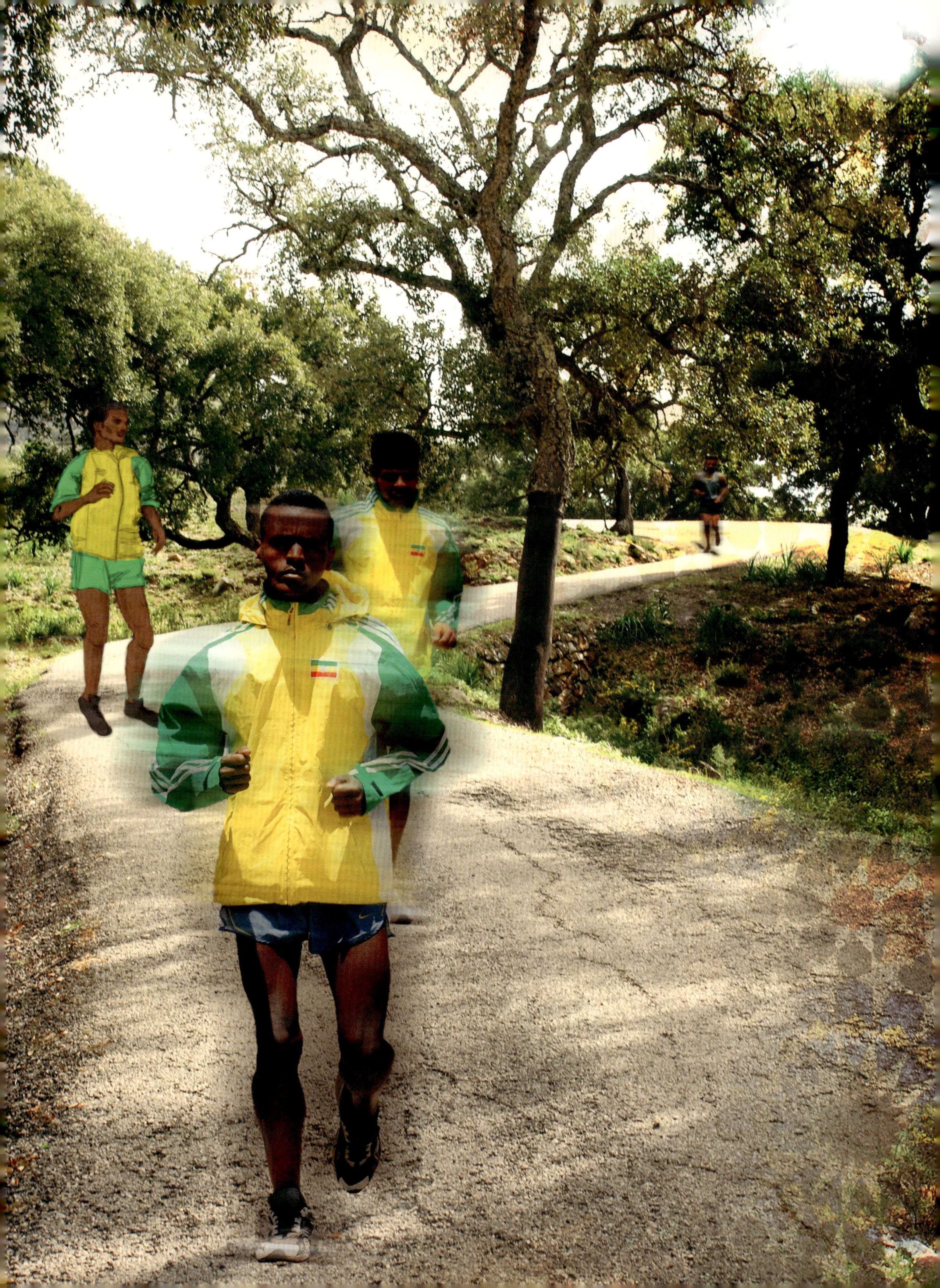

STOP! WHO ARE YOU AND WHY ARE YOU FOLLOWING US? KENYAN?
NO... I...
THEN WHY HAVE YOU BEEN FOLLOWING MY TRAINING SESSIONS FOR THE LAST THREE DAYS?
YOU SAW ME?
I SEE EVERYTHING! YOU'RE ETHIOPIAN?
YES, A RUNNER
A RUNNER? THEN LETS SEE IF YOU CAN KEEP UP...

WHAT'S YOUR NAME?

HAIKIM

WHERE ARE YOU FROM?

ASELA

THEN THERE'S SOME HOPE FOR YOU!

28:34 THAT'S GOOD. VERY GOOD. SAME TIME TOMORROW?

YES IF...

TRAINERS?

I PREFER NOT TO WEAR THEM

"WHO IS HE?"

RACING IS ART AND SCIENCE. SCIENCE ALLOWS YOU TO GET THE BEST FROM YOUR BODY.

THE ART COMES FROM WORKING AS A TEAM. THAT'S THE DIFFERENCE BETWEEN RUNNING AND RACING.

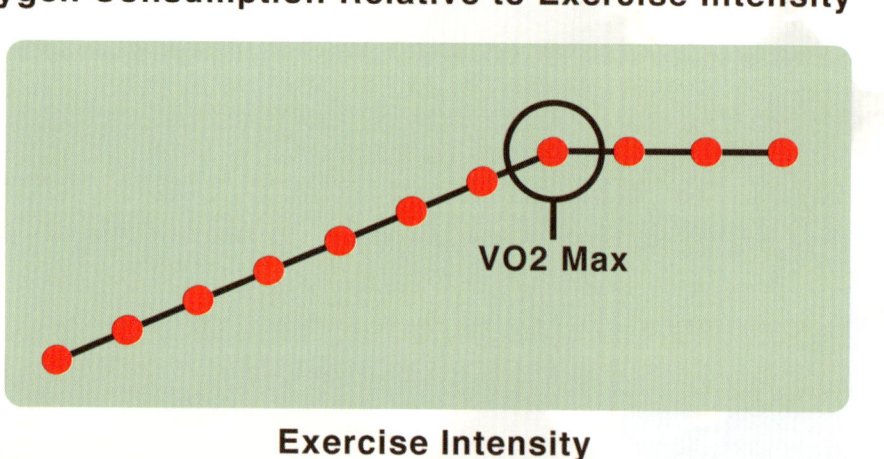

Oxygen Consumption Relative to Exercise Intensity

(Oxygen consumption vs. Exercise Intensity — VO2 Max)

THERE'S THE PACEMAKER

THE COMMUNICATOR

THE LEAD

"YOU'LL NEED TO BE A TEAM PLAYER TO WIN THE RACE HAIKIM."

Tangiers trial race

"HE'S GOOD, BUT WHOSE SIDE IS HE ON..."

"PACE YOURSELF HAIKIM!"

26:53 WHO IS THIS STRANGER?

"YOU CAN RUN HAIKIM. BUT YOU RUN ALONE."

"I DON'T DO IT ON PURPOSE, THAT'S JUST HOW I RUN."

"EVEN A CHEETAH MUST HAVE A MATE... SLOW DOWN HAIKIM FOR THE SAKE OF THE TEAM.

OH AND WEAR THE TRAINERS... YOU'LL GET USED TO THEM..."

"COACH WANTS TO SEE YOU... NOW."

Within weeks he had matched their times, after a month he was a rival for point runner. His time would come...

WHAT'S GOING ON?

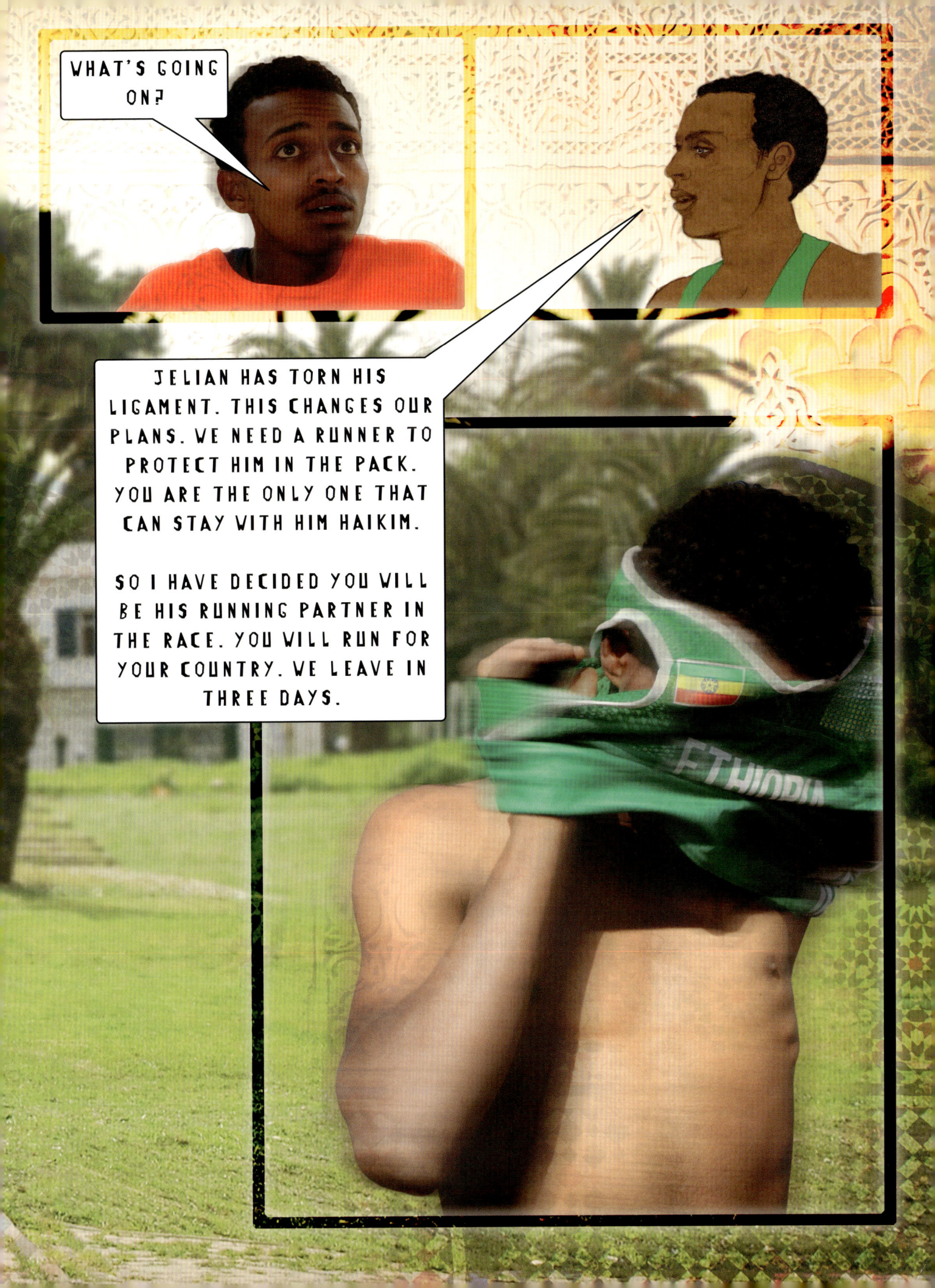

JELIAN HAS TORN HIS LIGAMENT. THIS CHANGES OUR PLANS. WE NEED A RUNNER TO PROTECT HIM IN THE PACK. YOU ARE THE ONLY ONE THAT CAN STAY WITH HIM HAIKIM.

SO I HAVE DECIDED YOU WILL BE HIS RUNNING PARTNER IN THE RACE. YOU WILL RUN FOR YOUR COUNTRY. WE LEAVE IN THREE DAYS.

10 Minutes to race

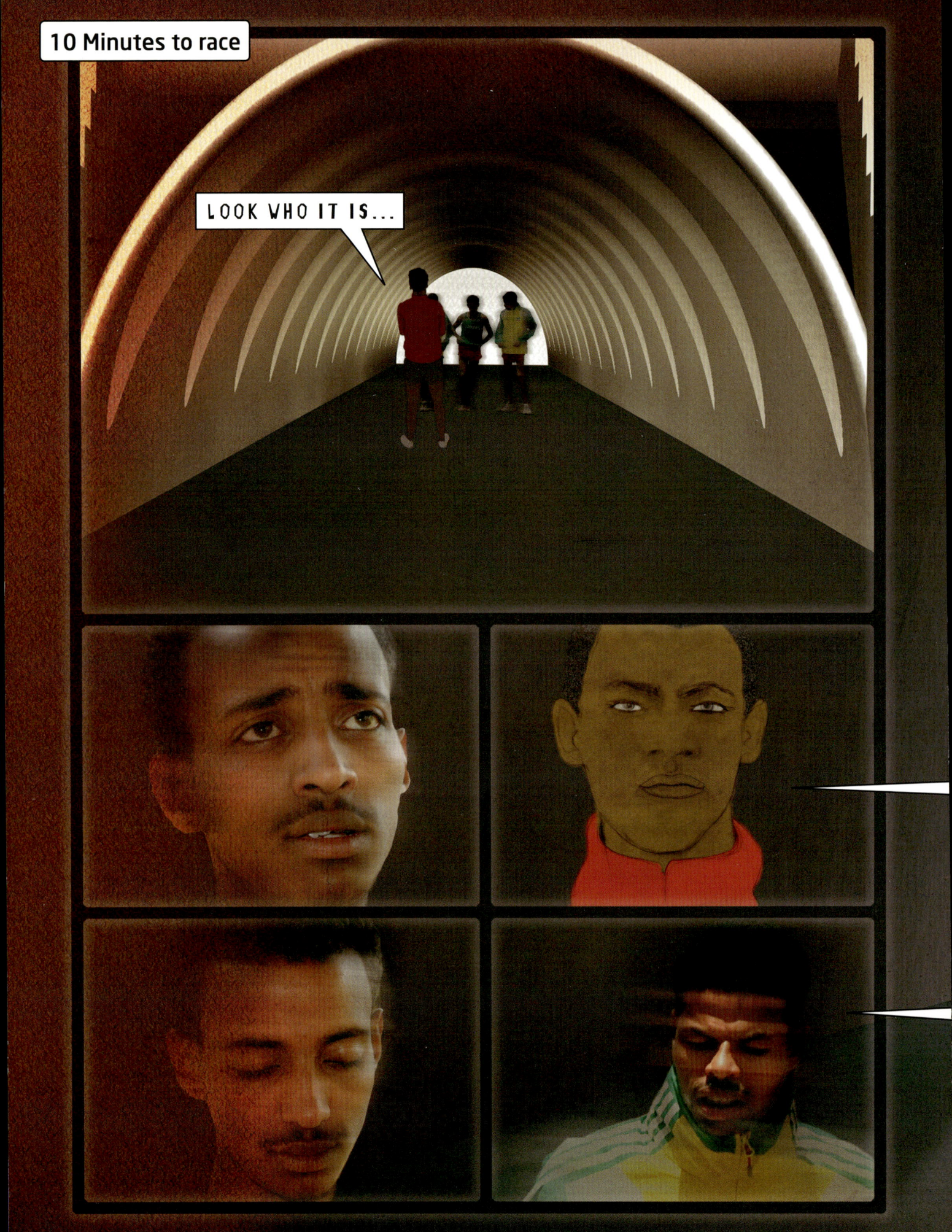

LOOK WHO IT IS...

> THE RUNNER WITH NO TRAINERS... YOU ARE A DISGRACE TO AFRICA. YOU MAKE US LOOK LIKE BEGGARS AND I WILL LEAVE YOU IN MY DUST.

> DON'T LISTEN TO THEM HAKIM. YOU RUN AS ONE OF US, BUT IT MAY BE A GOOD TIME TO PUT THE TRAINERS ON?

And they're off. This years much anticipated 10km race is finally under way. The big news being that the barefoot runner is no more - he's actually wearing trainers....
Yes I must say it's a bit of a disappointment after all the hype he's had in the build up to this race.

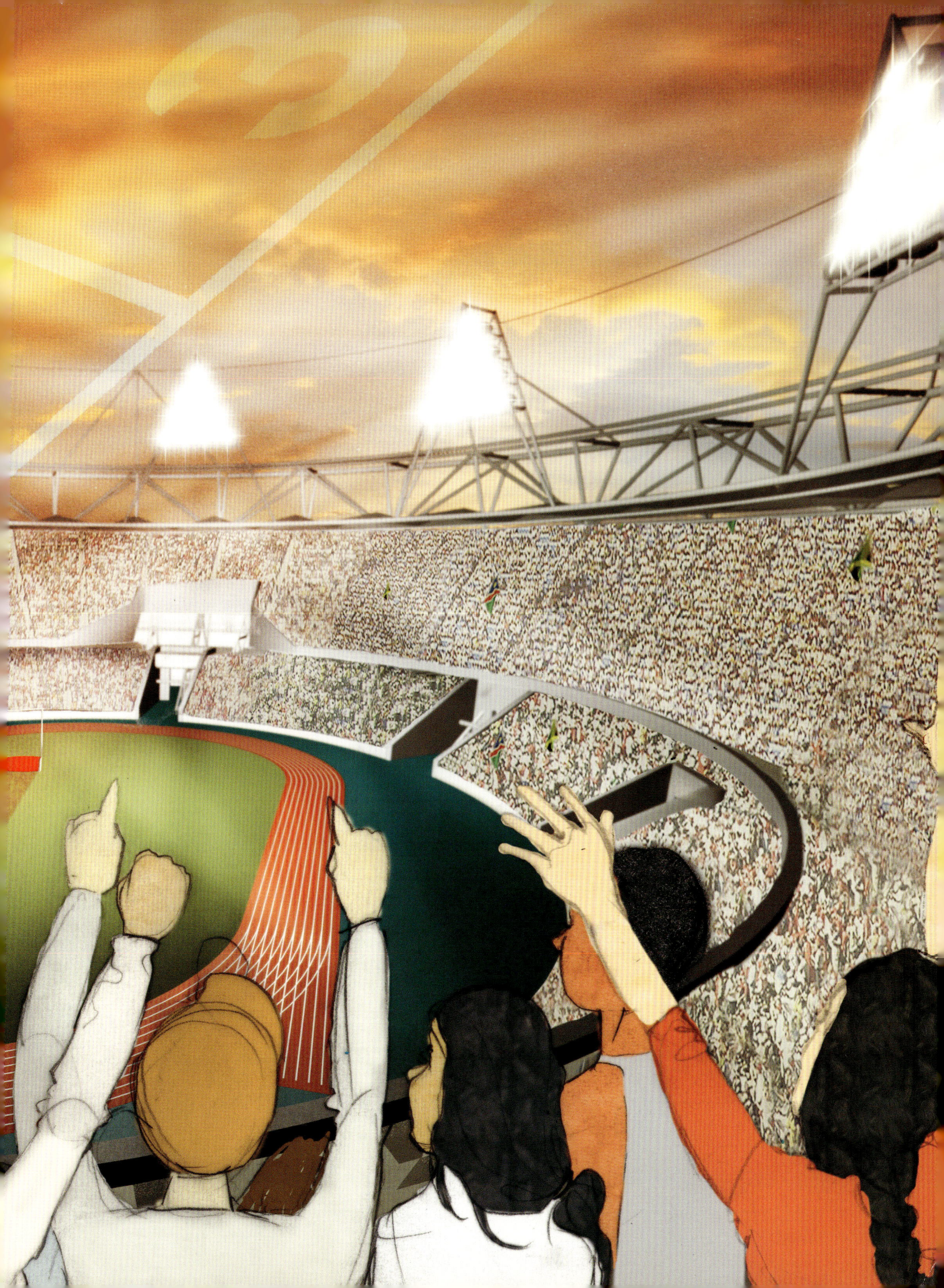

"The Kenyans are tight, Ethiopians working well as a unit so far."

"The jostling is starting and we can see Jelian being stepped and leaned on as they pass below."

"As we hit the half way mark we can see the Kenyans pulling away and the Ethiopians responding. The Lookie man takes a knock defending Jelian!"

Wait. They're down. Both Jelian and Lookie are down! Brought roughly to the ground by the Kenyan pack that's now pulling away into the distance.

The two runners are trying to get back up, but it seems Jelian simply cannot lift the leg that was injured a few weeks ago. What a tragedy for the Ethiopian team.

It seems Jelian is gesturing for his partner to join the chase but time is running out now surely. Wait...

Lookie is up on his feet and pleading with Jelian...

Now he's flung off his trainers...

"He's starting back after the pack and doing so at a furious pace."

"He may be feeling angry but surely he can't keep that pace up... he'll burn out by the next lap."

Can he really catch them from here?

The crowd seem to think so!

Yes! He's coming alongside them now. What a performance from this young man. The crowd is simply going wild as he passes on the outside. I've never seen anything like this before... I guess he just didn't read the rule book of racing because he's going straight past them with two laps to go. Can he keep it up? What a race...

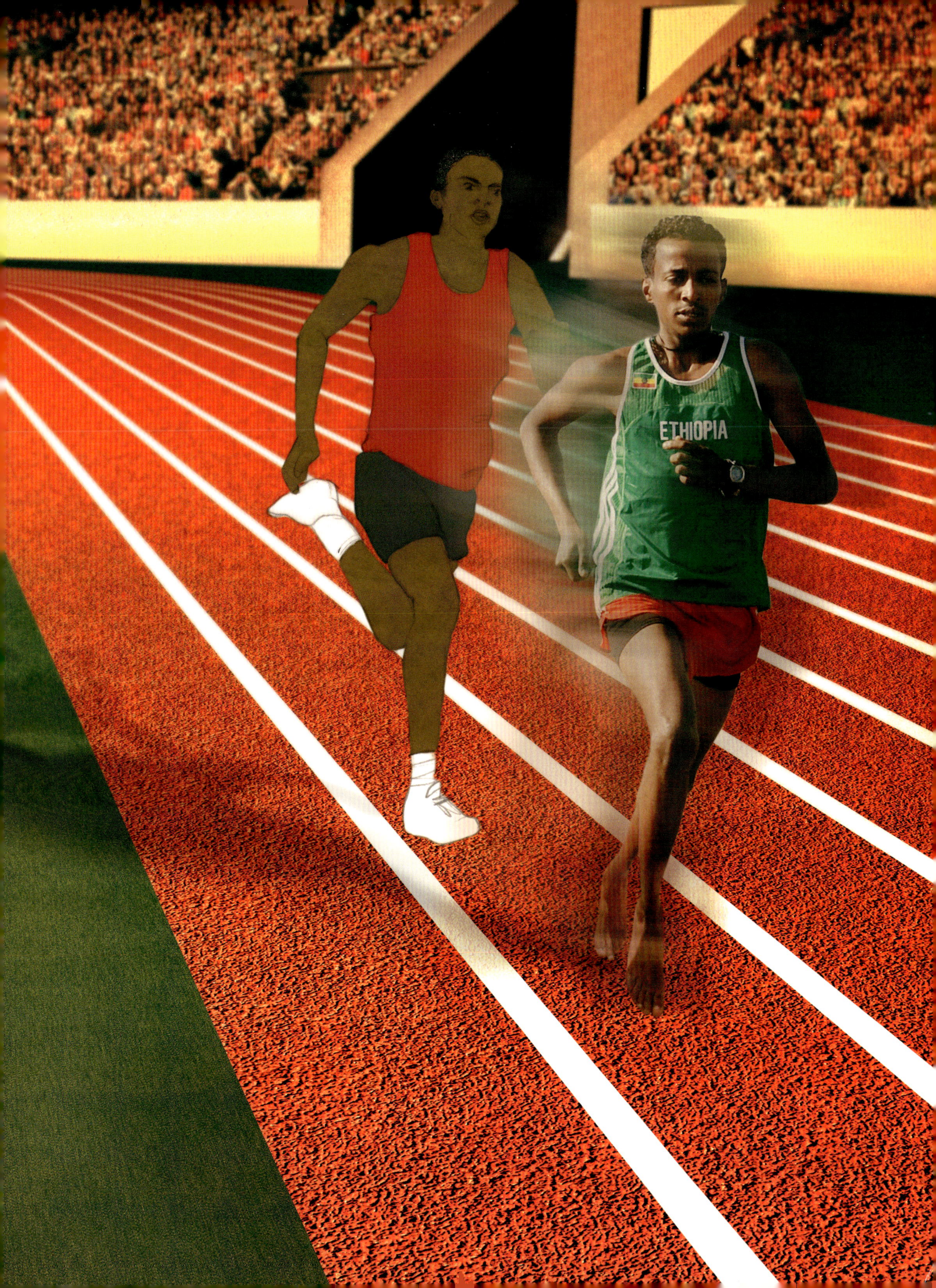
ETHIOPIA

The Kenyans are doing their best to stay with him but as as the bell rings it seems nobody has the legs to do it.

Unbelieveably the Olympic record is back within his reach as he enters the final lap. The noise here is immense. I can hardly hear myself speak.

He's cruising to the final bend and oh... he's slowing... Wait, he's stopping! I can't beleive it but he's stopped by Jelian.

"What is he doing!"

"Well if this wasn't incredible enough…"

The other runners are passing by and simply staring as Lookie and Bekele lift Jelian to his feet.

> Incredible scenes here in London as the crowd stand in ovation. The medals have been won, but everybody is watching these three walk the final straight. The Ethiopian flag draped across them.

Why did you stop Lookie? Are you injured? Is it a protest?
STOP RUNNING?
Yes why did you stop?
I'LL NEVER STOP
What do you mean?
I'VE BEEN RUNNING ALL MY LIFE. I'LL ALWAYS BE RUNNING.

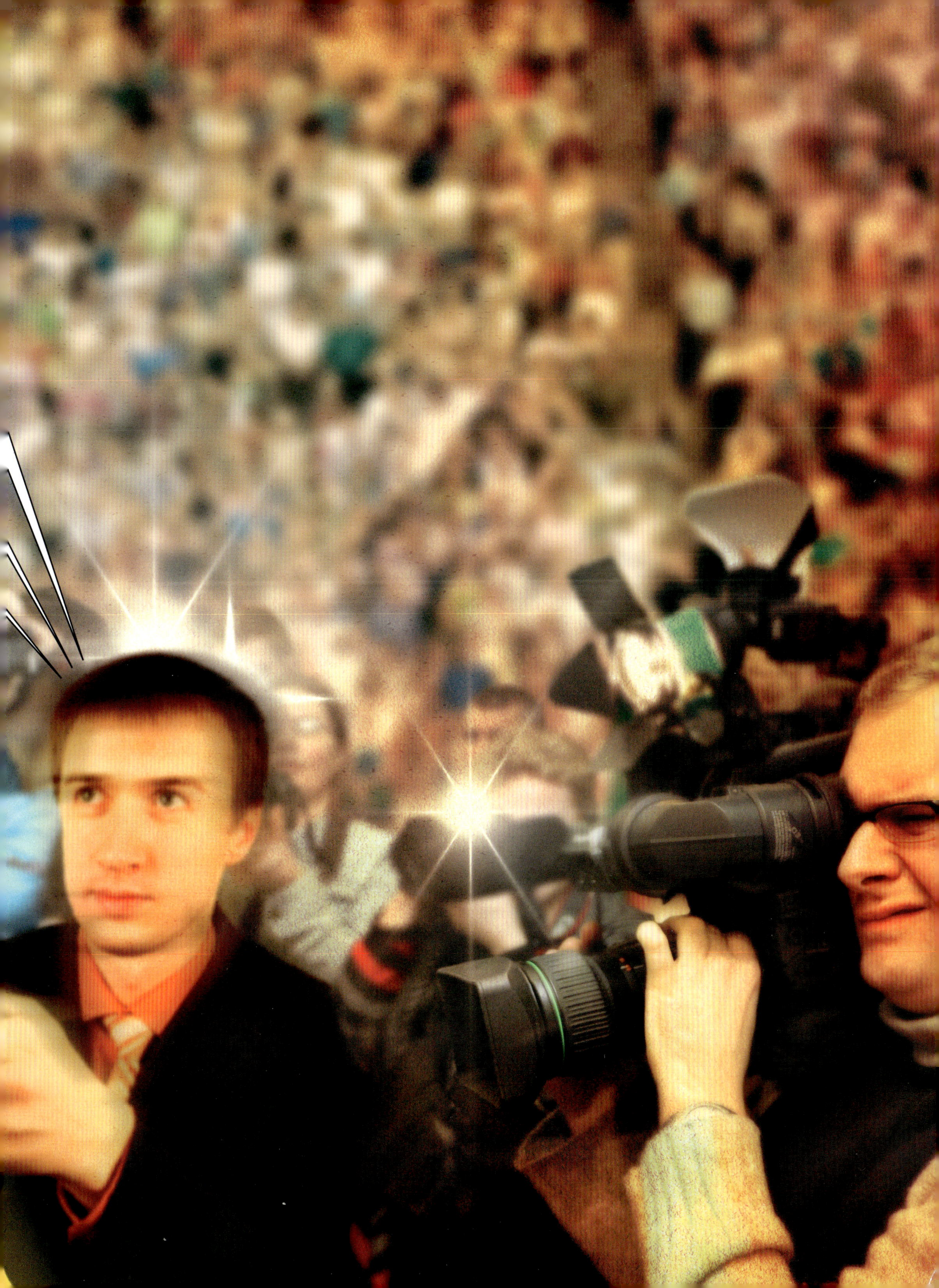

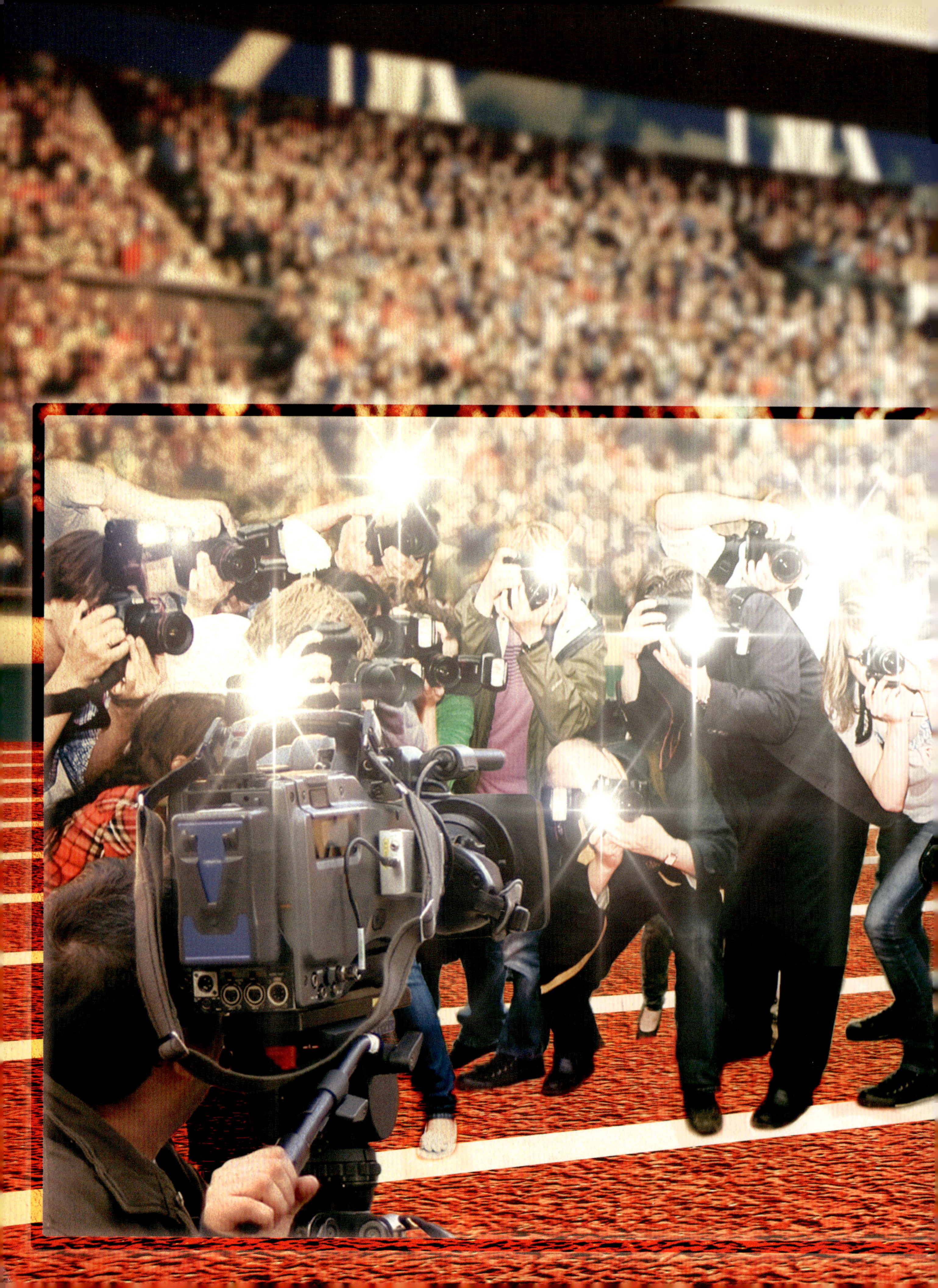

KILLI, THANK YOU BROTHER

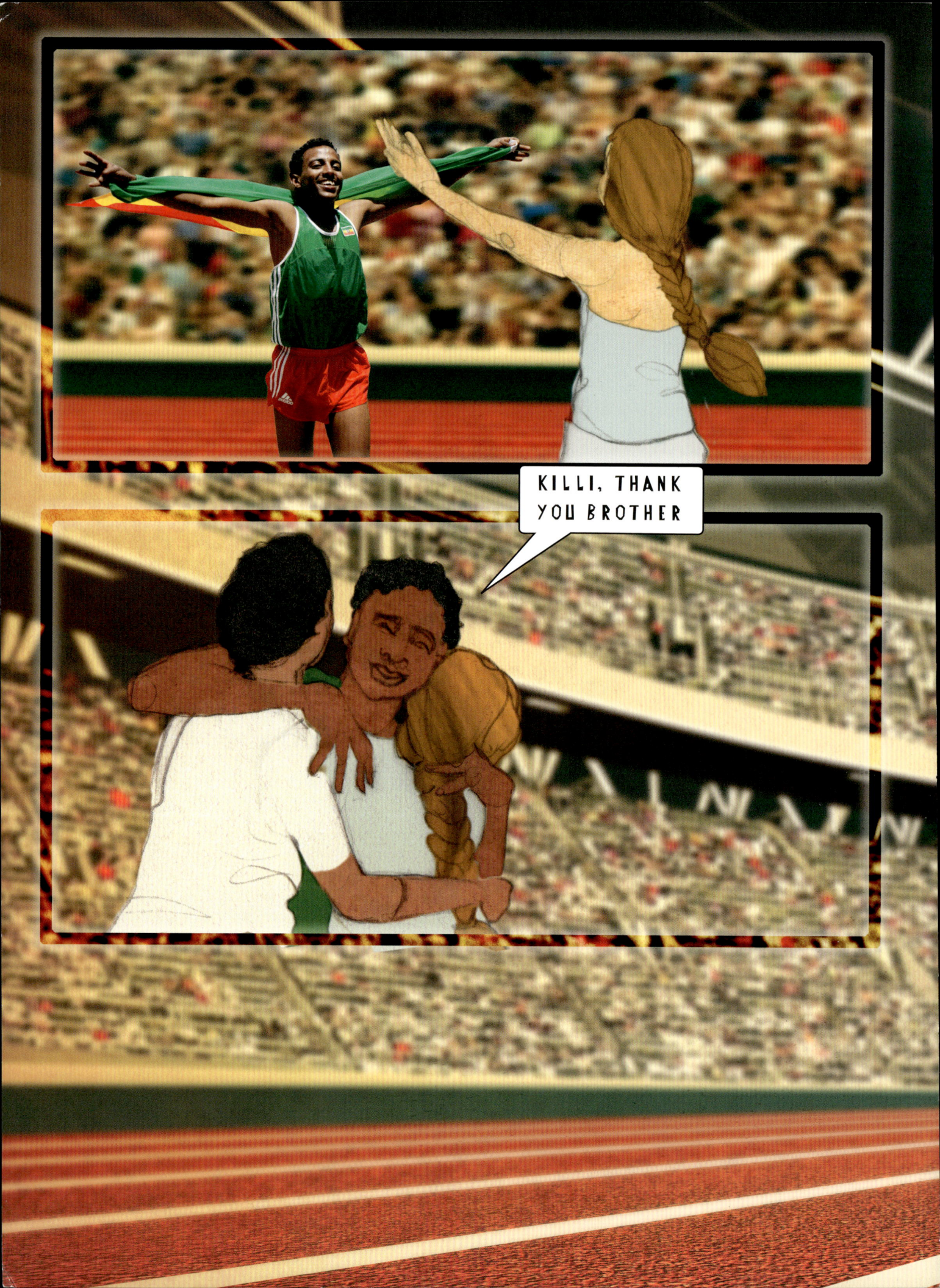

Always running; but now towards light, not shadow. A brief moment to burn brightly and remind others of the flame. This too shall pass.

Others are emerging. Crimson reds, flared oranges, burnt ocre. The flame spreads through their body in search of release.

It rises in all creeds, colours and continents. I see them from afar. I rise with them.